Cadoc

Geoffrey Malone spent most of his childhood in Africa and avoided any formal education until the age of eleven. After school in England, he spent sixteen years as a soldier, then joined a Canadian public relations firm in Toronto. During all this time, he travelled widely and developed a fascination with animals in the wild. He returned to Britain in 1991, determined to become a children's author.

He has written six books for children, each one with a powerful and closely-observed animal interest. His story of a fox, *Torn Ear*, won the 2001 French Children's Book of the Year Award and the Prix Enfants grands-parents Européen. In England, *Elephant Ben* was shortlisted for the 2001 Stockton Children's Book of the Year Award.

Cadoc is the result of almost a year's badger watching and research. It describes the recent criminal upsurge in badger baiting and the cruelty of humans towards these and other animals.

Cadoc

GEOFFREY MALONE

Hodder
Children's
Books

a division of Hodder Headline Limited

**To Ant and Jo Beattie,
in gratitude and friendship**

With grateful thanks to the following
for their knowledge and help:

Inspector Andy Fisher and Sergeant Hazel Collier,
of the Police Wildlife Crime Support Unit,
at New Scotland Yard.
Dr Elaine King and Susan Symes,
of the National Federation of Badger Groups.

One

The sack was small. Too small for the badger to turn around in. An old grey mail sack with sewn-in steel eyelets at one end, secured now with a heavy padlock. It held the badger in a vice-like grip that gave him no room to move. No way of escape.

The badger's feet scrabbled in vain against the smooth, unyielding sides. Claws that could slash through tree roots were of no use in here. The sack held him fast. And there was nothing to bite. Nothing for him to clamp his great jaws over and wrench and tear a way through. He was as helpless as a day-old rabbit.

He had been in here for over an hour. An hour of rage and frantic barking. The heat in the sack was suffocating. The plastic sides slippery and running with condensation. His head was rammed hard against the bottom of the bag where no fresh air reached. His fur was drenched in sweat.

His body sagged and he lay with his eyes closed. He was beaten. Trapped in a bewildering world of ugly new sounds and scents. The drumming of tyres on the road. The roar of the engine. And, most terrifying of all, the proximity of humans.

The smell of them was everywhere. A sweet, cloying odour that filled his nostrils and settled like a greasy film over his fur. He tried rubbing his tongue over his teeth to get rid of it, but the taste grew worse.

Flashes of recall began crowding in on him. A kaleidoscope of confusion, each image more frightening than the last. The sudden thump of men's boots overhead; the snarls of terriers running through the sett; spades slicing through the earth and the shouting and the noise as he was dragged out and his head rammed into the sack. And while he roared and fought, the terror of previous occupants rose to greet him. An acrid stink that screamed a terrible warning.

Panic-stricken, he hurled himself now against the sides of the sack, rolling over and over in a frenzy, while the brass padlock rapped a tattoo on the steel floor of the van. The men in the front of the van heard him and grinned at one another. 'He's a big strong boy, ain't he?' chuckled the driver. 'Take a good few dogs to sort him!'

His passenger agreed. 'Reckon they'll need to bust his jaw before the night's out. What's the betting?'

The driver shook his head. 'No takers! These old boars're all the same. Fight till they drop. It's the only thing they know.'

The other man reached behind his seat and pulled out a small iron bar. 'Can't hear m'self think with the row he's making!' He swung round and jabbed at the sack. 'Oi! You! Shut your row!'

He waited for a few more moments then brought the bar down hard. 'Shut it!' he shouted. He made a face and began to curse. 'Blasted thing's piddled itself!'

'So would you!' the driver joked and they both laughed. 'You try working in a slaughterhouse sometime,' he added and jerked a thumb over his shoulder. 'That there's nothing!'

The passenger didn't reply. Instead, he slouched back down in his seat and stared into the night. 'How much longer?' he grumbled. 'At this rate they'll all be gone home! Then there'll be trouble.'

'Can't go too fast on these little country roads,' the driver told him. 'Anyway, it's not that far now.' He gave a grunt a few minutes later as a signpost loomed up in the headlights. 'Might be this one. Funny how things look all different at night.'

He braked, changed gear and wound his window down. The night air rushed in, fogging his side of the windscreen. The driver peered out. 'Yeah! Spot on!' he called, satisfied. 'Not long now!' He flashed a grin at his passenger. 'Ten minutes? Give 'em a call on the mobile. Tell them to look out for us.'

The van's headlights carved a tunnel through the darkness. The ghostly shape of a barn owl flew ahead of them for a while then veered to one side and was swallowed up by the night. Sparkles of frost glittered on the road in front of them. The sound of the engine took on a new urgency.

The passenger slipped the mobile back into his pocket. 'Watch out for two red lights. One above the other. Oh! And take it easy when you get off the road,' he added. 'The track's all icy.'

They drove in silence, staring into the darkness beyond the headlights. Clumps of straggly trees rushed past and the grass glittered coldly. Behind them, they could hear the badger moaning quietly to itself.

'There they are!' the driver exclaimed. 'Two red lights like they said.' He flashed his headlights in acknowledgement then leant forward and carefully checked his wing mirrors. But there was no one following. He gave an involuntary sigh of relief and, for the first time that night, began to think of the money waiting for him.

He flashed the headlights once more and slowed to a walking pace. The van lurched as it swung off the road. Then they were crawling forward on sidelights only, squinting into the half-light. A shadowy figure appeared on the track beside them. He leant towards the driver's window, his face a pale blur. The air felt very cold. 'Watch your speed!' he ordered. 'You know where to go!' He banged the side of the van with a gloved fist and stamped his feet.

The driver gave him a thumbs-up and drove on slowly. Soon the track started to deteriorate. The men sat forward, hanging on grimly as the wheels crashed into potholes and churned through muddy ruts. In the back, the sack fetched up with a thump against the side of the vehicle.

'What's this place, then?' the passenger demanded.

'It's an old bomber base. World War Two. Or something.'

'Watch it!' the other man shouted as a huge pothole opened up in front of them.

The driver cursed and yanked at the steering

wheel. The engine raced. Dollops of mud sprayed the underside of the van as the rear wheels spun helplessly. The van slewed across the track towards a water-filled ditch. For a long moment nothing happened, then the tyres gripped and they bumped uncertainly on. The driver took a deep breath and puffed out his cheeks.

'The good news is that no one comes out here,' he resumed. 'It's that remote. Even for these parts.'

The passenger sniffed and wiped his nose across the back of his hand. 'Checked it out yourself, did you?'

The driver laughed. 'Dead right, I did! That's what I get paid for! It's the best!'

The passenger flung out an arm. 'Look! Over there! That's them! Great!' And he gave a whoop of relief.

A light was flashing on and off in front of them. Now the track gave way to smoother concrete. The vehicle accelerated. Low buildings began to appear on either side. There were vehicles parked alongside most of them.

The passenger rubbed his hands in delight. 'Full house! Looks like all the lads have come.'

They stopped below the airfield's old control tower. It was a two-storey brick building with a set of stairs leading up the outside to what had been the observation platform. The windows were long gone. Now they were just jagged spaces staring out over silent runways. High above the van, a man with a pair of night binoculars round his neck stared down.

Beside them, a door was flung open and yellow light flooded across the tarmac. The night was suddenly full of men. Big burly figures who crowded round, grinning with delight. Shoulders were slapped and a whisky bottle was thrust into the driver's hand. Inside the building, a dog began to bark.

The driver went round to the back of the van and tugged open the doors. The men bunched together in a tight semicircle, watching. The sack lay in the middle of the floor. There was a loud sigh from the watchers. A slow release of anticipation. The sack bulged as the badger tried to stand. He knew the men were there.

And the dogs waiting inside. He could hear them and smell their hate.

Strong hands grabbed the sack and bundled it inside. They hurried it along a brick corridor where the weeds grew out of cracks. A door was flung open into a large windowless room. There were electric lights overhead, hanging down on long flexes. Straw bales were piled in one corner.

A hoarse cheer went up. More men followed, crowding in after them. Some had muzzled dogs on short steel leads, held in close. Now the straw bales were being lifted out and stacked three high to form a ring. Money was pulled from back pockets and battered wallets. Odds were shouted and taken. There was laughter. Someone dropped a bottle. There was a cheer and good-natured cursing. Everyone seemed to know each other.

The driver clapped his hands over his head and shouted for silence. He was a heavy-set man with thick black eyebrows. The door banged shut. A hush fell. Eyes gleamed. He took a key from his jacket pocket and squatted down. Carefully, he placed the padlock on the floor beside him. Then he swung the sack up on to his shoulder and walked towards the bales. He looked round the room. 'Everyone ready!'

With a grin of triumph, he upended the sack. There was a deafening shout. The badger fell tail first on to the concrete floor. For a split second, it lay motionless, blinded by the light. Then the first two dogs erupted into his face and his world became a snarling, biting bloodlust.

Two

Marla froze. There was something outside. Something listening. Waiting. Not another badger; it had moved too quietly for that. The sound of a foot brushing against an old leaf, then silence. The silence that falls when animals stand stiff and motionless, straining to hear. But above all, it was a warning. A threat to her three cubs, and something she must deal with. Right away.

She heard a cub whimper in the darkness behind her and knew the intruder would have heard it too. She was not frightened for herself. Humans were the only animal a badger feared. But for an instant, she was terrified for her cubs. The three helpless, silky-haired little creatures curled up deep in the pile of dry grass that filled the nursery chamber, five metres along the passage.

She squinted at the tunnel entrance. Outside the sett, it was a world of brilliant moonlight. So bright, she could hardly bear to look at it. She lifted her head and slowly moved it from side to side, smelling the night air. She took a silent step towards the glare and caught the faintest whiff of stale urine. And then she knew!

A fox. An old dog fox. No threat to her but certain death to her cubs. She had lost a cub from her first litter to a fox the year before. And now the memory came flooding back. Her fur bristled as rage swept through her. She burst out of the tunnel entrance in a fury. The fox leapt to one side, screaming in shock. The badger was already spinning round and coming for him.

Marla lunged for his back, her mouth wide open. The fox dodged to one side. He knew that one bite from those terrible jaws would crush his spine and leave him helpless. But he was not quite quick enough. Marla's claws ripped at his ribs and he staggered and almost fell. Blood welled along the slash marks. For a moment, the pain transfixed him and he was fighting for breath, unable to move, watching stupidly as the badger ran at him again.

Somehow, instinct came to his rescue and he was ducking away from the sow, skidding across the ground and off down the hillside, leaping over briar tangles, dodging past stands of saplings, to the safety of the open fields, far below.

Marla plunged after him, snorting in triumph. She chased him most of the way down before reluctantly realizing that he was still too fast for her. She waited until the sound of his yelps finally died away, then turned to make her way back. It was a steep climb but her powerful legs made short work of it.

Near the sett, a woodmouse shot across her path barely a metre away, its ears flat against its skull. Marla heard its terrified squeaking and saw the weasel in pursuit. It took the weasel a split second to turn its head, see the badger and leap out of the way. But it was just enough time for the mouse to dodge into a tuft of grass and squeeze inside its tiny burrow. The weasel stood on its hind legs and chattered with rage as Marla lumbered past.

When she reached the sett, Marla went inside. The cubs were still fast asleep. She bent over them and reassured herself that they were still warm. Satisfied, she went further back along the tunnel and listened for any sign of the rest of her family. There was none. Cadoc, her mate for the past two years, and their three almost fully grown cubs from the previous year were still out foraging. None of them would return until the dawn. And that was still some hours away.

She had deliberately waited for Cadoc to leave the sett first. She would not allow the boar anywhere near the nursery until the new cubs were big enough to fend for themselves. A jealous male would kill his cubs without hesitation. That was Nature's way. In ten weeks' time or so, they would all feed and play together as a family, and the danger would be over. But until then, she would take no risks.

Every night as it grew dark, she waited for Cadoc to lead the others out to feed. He would stand just inside one of the many entrances to the sett and peer out. The yearlings would wait impatiently in the tunnel behind him. When he was satisfied it was safe to leave, she would hear his grunt and the sounds of the others following him.

She heard the sudden bad-tempered shrilling of a blackbird. Had the fox come back? Furious, she shot out into the moonlight, her teeth bared. Above her, the bird scolded her mate, then puffed up her feathers against the cold. Marla listened intently while the bird settled back into the nest and went to sleep. There was no sign of the fox and she knew then it would not return that night.

But there was something else. A faint scuffling noise from somewhere under her feet. She recognized the sound immediately. It was a mole, digging. The sound of earth spraying against the sides of its tunnel was unmistakable. She stared at the ground in front of her and mentally followed its progress. It was too far down, she decided, to waste time digging for it now. Instead, she would wait for it to surface and catch it then.

She sat on her haunches and began to groom herself, licking her fur and combing it back into place with her long fore claws. Next, she scratched herself all over. It was a wonderful feeling and she began to purr with pleasure. When she had finished, she shook herself and fluffed out her fur. A cloud drifted across the moon and cast a shadow over the clearing. She looked up at the night sky and realized with a shock that time was passing and that she had still not fed.

This worried her. She was much later than usual. The fox had distracted her for far longer than she had realized. The cubs would be waking soon and demanding their feed. She had to eat to go on providing the hourly milk they needed. But if she wasn't there, they'd soon become frantic and start losing body heat. And once that started to happen they would all soon die.

She began to fret, running backwards and forwards in short rushes, uncertain what to do. She was suddenly hungry. Very hungry. She could wait no longer. Snorting with impatience, she put her head down and cast round for the scent path that would lead to her favourite feeding ground. The next moment, she was bustling along it, grunting loudly, oblivious of everything else.

Three

Cadoc stood in the shadow of a hedgerow, listening intently. Far off across the fields, he heard the roar of a car starting up. He stiffened. He knew that sound. It meant danger. He stared into the night, searching for the warning flash of headlights. Ready to sink down into the ditch and hide while the creature rushed past, bellowing in anger.

He waited motionless for a couple more minutes, then, satisfied he had outwitted it, he trotted across the field towards an oak tree. There were always acorns to be found half-hidden in the earth. He stopped several times on his way there to raise his tail and mark the larger tussocks of grass with his scent.

It was Cadoc's task, as the dominant male, to patrol the boundaries of the fifty hectares of field and woodland the family occupied and warn all other males to keep out. He did this every night, trotting purposefully around the perimeter, marking the boundary between his territory and that of his neighbours.

He paused every ten metres or so to spray or scent prominent tussocks, stones, tree stumps or posts. It took him several hours to do and he took even greater care now Marla was nursing cubs. Between his territory and his neighbour's, there was a no-man's land, a metre wide. An invisible barrier of smell, a warning to every other badger, not to cross.

But not tonight! Not now! Something strange was happening. Cadoc stopped scratching up acorns and stood transfixed. He had caught the faintest of scents. A taste that brought him up short and made his mouth water. The scent was too fragile to last long on the night air. Yet powerful enough to bring him running down towards the old wooden stile at the far end of the field.

Apples! The unmistakable fragrance of apples. Last year's harvest, with the sugar concentrated deep inside their puckered skins. He had passed this spot a thousand times but had never found this scent before.

When he reached the stile he stopped and stood rigid with concentration, trying to pinpoint the source. It had been there. He was certain. And he knew the direction it had come from. His first instinct was to hurry towards it. But he hesitated. There were other things to consider.

Such as the short-tempered, grizzled old badger whose territory he would have to cross first. Cadoc was a strong and healthy four-year-old. He was almost a metre long from nose to tail. He was powerfully built with a broad head and a thick, muscular neck. But Findar, the old boar, whose territory it was, was more than a match for him. And Cadoc knew it.

Findar weighed close to twelve kilograms and, unusually for a badger, was always spoiling for a fight. Cadoc remembered a recent attack he had made on a young male trespasser and shivered. He had heard the screams and later seen the intruder dragging himself along with a useless and mangled back leg. He had listened to the animal's sobs for a very long time before they faded into the dawn.

Yet despite this, the fact was that somewhere not far away, there were apples. Lots and lots of apples. And the thought of them tormented him. He put his head on one side and listened. An owl was beating backwards and forwards searching for food. It was old and its wing joints were stiff. He could hear the wind slipping through its ragged feathers. Soon it would be too old to hunt and a fox would find it lying on the ground, unable to fly up into its tree. But there was no sound anywhere of another badger.

He took a step towards the stile. Then another. The warning scent from Findar's markings rose to meet him, impossible to ignore. They were stark and brutal. Cadoc closed his eyes and remembered the bites he had seen on the young badger's legs. One more step and he too would be inside Findar's territory.

He wanted to turn back but somehow his mouth was full of the taste of scrunched-up apples. It was too much. Grunting with determination and quite a lot of fear, he squeezed under the stile and ran across the meadow into the darkness beyond.

Four

Marla, meanwhile, was following her nose along the path that led to 'Twenty Acre' field. It was a route all the family used and had been scented by generations of badgers. In human terms, it was rather like following 'cat's eyes' along a main road at night. As she bustled along, she knew Cadoc and the others had come this way much earlier.

Overhead, the weather was changing. Thin clouds were beginning to stream across the face of the moon. The air was noticeably warmer and it began to drizzle. Soon the ground in front of her glistened with damp. Marla was delighted. The rain would bring the earthworms wriggling up to the surface.

And worms were her favourite food.

She reached the edge of the field and stopped. The previous October, the field had been planted with spring wheat. It was now well over shoulder height and gave excellent cover. By now, raindrops were starting to slide down the wheat stalks. The drizzle grew heavier. It turned to rain and beat a summons the worms could not resist.

All around her she knew thousands of earthworms were rushing upwards. Soon, she could hear the air quivering with a new sound. Faint at first but growing louder all the time. A dry, slithery noise as the worms wriggled back up their tunnels towards the rain. Then the faint 'pop' as their heads broke the surface.

Marla gave a whicker of delight and licked her lips. But she made herself wait a little longer until she was sure the worms would all be out in the open. Only then did she walk slowly forward with her snout just brushing the ground.

There were worms everywhere, sliding over the damp earth, rolling from side to side in delight, oblivious to everything. She picked one up between her teeth. The worm's tail immediately gripped the edge of its tunnel and hung on. It was surprisingly strong.

Carefully, Marla pulled it upright, then stopped. She knew from experience that a sudden tug would lose her half the worm. And she hadn't any time to waste. There was however an infallible way to catch worms. It was a trick her mother had taught her when she had been a cub.

Still holding the worm, Marla began tickling it with the hairs on the back of her paw. The worm shivered up and down its length, then abruptly let go. Greedily, she sucked it down.

She fed for the next twenty minutes, smacking her lips in pleasure after each worm. She nibbled experimentally at a head of wheat but found it still green and bitter. Then, she decided it was time to return to the sett. She was still hungry and could easily have eaten another hundred worms. Normally she would have done, but tonight she was impatient to get back. With a bit of luck she might find a family of slugs on the way there.

As she recrossed 'Twenty Acre' field, she came across the scent of the dog fox again. It was fresh. So fresh, it was impossible to know whether he had sprayed the ground just before she had chased him away. Or . . . after! She stopped dead as the terrible thought struck her. What if the old fox had outwitted her? Could he have doubled back towards the sett? Knowing she thought she had seen him off? Had he been lying up somewhere close, just waiting for her to leave?

She began to run. The fox might be in the sett at this moment. Seizing one of the cubs in his jaws. She gave a frantic bark and raced back up the hill, her mind in a turmoil. A hedgehog hearing her coming curled up tightly into a ball and held its breath. Marla rushed past too panic-stricken to even notice it.

She crashed through the undergrowth regardless of the noise she made. She was sure she had chased that fox off for a very long time. She remembered the painful way it had run from her. She had hurt it. And yet. . . . The worry closed in on her.

She tried to remember all she knew about foxes. They were unpredictable, and clever. They so often did the unexpected – it was all part of their hunting skills. Usually both species tolerated each other. Only last year, a vixen had taken over a tunnel in the sett and then given birth to four cubs. At first the badgers had grumbled amongst themselves, but they made no effort to evict them. After a couple of months, when the smell became too bad, the badgers had moved to another part of the sett, still complaining.

Later, in the summer, after the foxes had finally left, Cadoc and the others had returned and spent many hours cleaning out the debris of old droppings and half-chewed bones which the foxes had left behind.

It was raining hard by the time she reached the sett. She burst out of the trees and ran towards the entrance, dreading what she might find. With jaws wide open, she plunged inside.

The sound of hungry cubs greeted her. All

three of them were awake and crying bitterly. Whimpering with relief, she rolled them over to make sure they were unharmed. Then she licked their faces and little blind eyes in a surge of love.

She shook herself vigorously and climbed on top of the grass bed. She lay on her side and called them. The two larger cubs were already nuzzling her, their tiny mouths fastening on her teats. The runt of the litter was struggling to reach her, wailing loudly as it kept sinking into the soft bedding.

Tenderly, she stretched out a large paw and scooped him to her. She waited, watching his head turning feebly, then pulled him hard against her stomach. She dropped back and closed her eyes. Her heart was still racing but she no longer cared. A feeling of intense pleasure flooded through her and she fell asleep almost at once.

Five

Cadoc flung a glance over his shoulder and wheezed in alarm. Perhaps it was only a shadow he had seen. It might just have been a bush. But it had looked like a badger and he had this dreadful feeling that Findar was after him. Stalking him. Waiting for the right moment to attack!

The only way to find out for sure was to stop and listen. But the thump of his own heart filled his head and drowned every other sound. By the time he heard Findar coming, it would be too late and he would have thrown away any chance of escape.

Instead, Cadoc ran even faster and was so preoccupied, he almost went tumbling headlong down a steep bank into the river that ran a long way below him. Snorting in alarm, he scrambled back up to the top of the bank and stared down. He had not been expecting this.

It was raining again and the shadows had all disappeared. Cadoc crouched down and waited. A minute went by and another. Gradually, he began to hear the sounds the river was making. Perhaps it had only been his imagination after all. Feeling better, he got to his feet and stared down at the surface.

He watched the waterweed streaming out in the current. He tried to judge the strength of the flow, knowing he would have to cross it. Not far away, a moorhen squawked and began beating her wings in real distress. There was a loud splash then silence.

He tensed and listened hard. She had been fast asleep on her nest of sticks. So what had attacked her? A fox? A stoat? Or perhaps a large male badger looking for eggs. Cadoc didn't wait any longer. He slipped down the bank and eased into the water. The current pushed against his side, turning him in the direction of the moorhen. He dug deep with his back legs and swam steadily at an angle towards the far bank.

He found a place where the ground had been trampled by cattle and pulled himself up. He stopped to shake the water out of his coat then made his way through a patch of dead nettle stalks. A rabbit thumped the ground in warning and all around him there was a flurry of movement. White scuts flickered as the does rushed to their burrows in panic. He heard the faint cries of their young under his feet and for a moment was tempted.

It wouldn't take long to dig down to a nest with its tiny pink occupants. He paused, aware of the commotion he was causing, then decided to leave the warren behind. He could always come back to it. He ducked through a hedge and found himself in a waterlogged meadow where his feet made little squelching noises as he hurried along. He stopped beside a clump of grass.

A dog had been here earlier that night.

Cadoc sniffed at it again. Dogs did not frighten him whatever their size. He was more than a match for any dog in a straight fight. But dogs were human allies and their presence was a warning. Wherever they were, humans would be close behind. He cast around and found more dog scents. They seemed to be everywhere. He hurried on.

A row of trees loomed up in front of him and the warm smell of cows was suddenly all around him. It filled his nostrils and he sneezed. He turned his head this way and that, trying to avoid it. The smell blanketed out everything else. Even the scent of humans. Foxes often rolled in cow dung before they went hunting. It disguised their own scent. He had often seen them do it.

He ran off to one side and kept upwind of the smell. Fifty metres further on, he came to a stone wall, where he stopped. He ran along the foot of the wall and found a place where the stone had collapsed. He clambered up and looked around.

There were high buildings with slate roofs

ahead. Barns and outhouses full of hay and turnips. Cadoc stood entranced. There were rats and large families of mice. He could hear them running under the straw bales. The smell of dogs was strong again. And something else. A scent that made him moan. Apples! He had found them.

He rushed forward in triumph, forgetful of everything. He squeezed between the bars of an old wooden gate, his belly brushing over the mud left there that morning by the farmer's boots. Yittering with excitement, he ran across the yard past an open-sided barn. A cat saw him coming and arched her back, spitting at him as he rushed past.

A rat ran across in front of him. It turned to look at him and the next moment was racing for its life over the greasy concrete. Cadoc ran on, all his concentration centred on a long, wooden shed where the smell of apples was overpowering.

But when he got there, he could find no way in. He ran up and down in mounting frustration, searching for a hole to squeeze through. But found nothing. He started to dig, his claws ripping at the concrete foundations. And found to his fury that they were making no impression at all.

Baffled, he battered his head against the side of the shed and felt it tremble. He stared at the wood and examined it more closely. After a while he found what looked like a long, thin crack. It ran straight above his head. He peered at it and slipped the tips of his claws inside. He felt it move a fraction then stick. He tugged at it, harder this time. Again it moved and with a slight bang this time. He looked up and saw the wooden latch.

Puzzled, Cadoc stared at it for a moment. He stood up and knocked it with the side of his paw. The door trembled. He hit it again and as the door swung back, he stumbled and almost fell inside. A warm gush of air met him and for a moment he felt giddy.

A wide shelf ran all the way round the walls. He stood on tiptoe, holding on to it with both paws, and peered at the fruit. He stretched out an arm and seized an apple. And another. And several more after that. His eyes closed in total bliss as the juice dripped down his chest. Then he realized the rest of them were out of reach.

He stretched across the shelf as far as he could but it was no use. The nearest apple was still a couple of centimetres beyond him. He tugged at the shelf. Nothing happened. In a rage, he banged his fist down hard and an apple started to roll towards him, then stopped.

He lifted his feet off the ground and swung from the shelf. It creaked. Encouraged, he jumped up and hooked his chin and elbows over the shelf and pressed down. At the fourth attempt, he heard the soft splintering of old wood. He did it again, this time trying to get his whole body on top of it.

There was a loud bang. The legs gave way and the shelf tipped over. Apples rolled across the floor in a giant cascade. Whimpering like a cub, Cadoc chased them and stuffed them into his mouth.

Six

'But who left the shed door open?' Mrs Jeferson demanded. She sounded cross. 'I know I put it on the latch last night.' She looked accusingly at the twins, who crowded into the doorway behind her. 'Were either of you out here before you went to bed?'

Tom shook his head and nudged Sarah, his sister. Anything that delayed going to school was all right by him. They had both been about to leave and catch the school bus when their father, Steve Jeferson, had put his head round the kitchen door and called, 'Someone's scoffed all the apples! Come and have a look!'

Sarah glared at her mother. 'Mum!' She sounded shocked. 'Of course we weren't!' She was a tall girl of thirteen. Like Tom, she had a mop of red hair. 'Besides, what's there to want out here?'

'Just some sad old apples,' said Tom.

'And you only ever used them to make sauce with,' Sarah reminded her.

'That's not the point!' Joyce Jeferson snapped, her eyes gleaming behind her glasses. 'Someone's been in here and deliberately broken that shelf!'

'It was rotten anyway,' Tom told her with a grin.

'Always has been,' Sarah agreed. 'Perhaps it just sort of collapsed.'

'Might have been a fox,' suggested Tom. 'What do you think, Dad?'

Steve Jeferson shook his head. He was a ruddy-faced man with deep laughter lines around his eyes. Right now, he looked puzzled. 'A fox would eat the apples all right. No doubt about that. But . . .' He bent down and dragged out a piece of splintered wood. 'It's not got the weight to do this.'

There was an indignant bark and Buster,

Steve's little dog, squeezed inside to see what was happening. He looked up at them all in turn, wagging his stumpy tail in greeting. Then he put his head on one side and stared at the plank Steve was holding. He took it in his jaws and gently pulled it away from Steve. Then, growing bolder, he began to worry it, growling happily to himself.

'So what was it, then?' Joyce demanded.

Steve didn't say anything. Instead, he looked at Sarah and gave her a friendly wink. He pushed past the twins and began to examine the outside of the door, peering closely at it. Then he chuckled and sat back on his heels.

'See these!' He ran a finger up and down the door. 'Claw marks. Big uns!'

They looked over his shoulder, staring at the deep scratches. 'And look here!' he called, pointing at the ground. 'See his tracks? Those five big toe marks. And see how much longer the middle two claws are?'

He looked up at the twins in triumph. 'Know what it is?'

'Not a fox?' ventured Tom.

Steve shook his head. 'Think about it! They're way too big for a fox. No! Looks like old Brock himself came visiting. We should be honoured.'

'A badger!' the twins exclaimed in delight.

'That's him all right!' Steve pushed his cap back and grinned. 'We had a badger here when I was a child,' he told them. 'Only a cub, mind. During that bad winter in '63. My dad found it. We kept it in the kitchen by the fire. Your grandmother used to feed it milk from one of my old baby bottles! It used to follow her around like a puppy. Then one day, it went. Never saw it again.'

'Do you think something got it?' Tom asked.

Steve made a face.

'But who left the door open?' Joyce Jeferson insisted. 'I shut it. I can distinctly remember doing it.'

'Clever animals, badgers,' Steve told her getting to his feet. 'That latch of yours wouldn't have kept him out for long.'

Sarah wrinkled her nose. 'But how did he open it?'

Steve put his hand on the latch. 'See these streaks of mud? That's where he reached up for it. The mud's from his paws. Then, he just knocked it down, same as you would.' He rubbed his chin. 'First time we've had a Brock in the yard for years.'

'Where's he from?' Tom asked.

His father shrugged. 'Used to be a sett in those woods on the hill. Looked abandoned last time I was up there. Maybe I'll go and take another look.'

'Can I come?' the twins asked simultaneously.

Joyce frowned. 'Well, I hope it's going to stay up there. I don't want it coming and scrounging round here every night.' She looked hard at Steve. 'Besides, they're a danger to cattle. Spreading TB and diseases. We don't want any more vets' bills. We can't afford them. Or had you forgotten?'

Steve shrugged. 'Nothing's ever been proved against them,' he told her. 'And our cattle are all beef. So we're OK. Besides,' he added, smiling at the twins, 'I like badgers.'

'Oh, for heaven's sake!' Joyce interrupted.

'Look at the time! You're both going to be really late! And I've got this new manager poking round the office today. Come on, you two. Get in the car! I'll drop you off.'

Tom looked at his watch and grinned. With a bit of luck they'd have missed the usual bus. And the next one was sure to get stuck in the rush hour in the local town. He bent over the badger's paw marks to have another look, then sauntered towards the car.

Steve waved a hand at them and turned away. 'Come on, dog!' he called. 'Let's make a start.' A few minutes later, he was busy loading bales of hay into the back of the ancient Land-Rover.

Seven

Later that night, Steve Jeferson stood at the bar of the village pub. It had been a bad day. Just before lunch, a calf had developed a fever and he'd had to wait five hours before the vet could get to him. By that time, the animal was in great distress and it was touch and go whether it would survive. Then Eric, his only farm-hand, had injured himself jumping down and landing heavily on an unseen nail in a plank of wood. The plank was lying in the mud and the six-inch nail had gone straight through his boot, piercing the foot. He would be off work for at least three weeks. Probably more.

'And it couldn't have come at a worse time,' Steve thought gloomily. There were going be a lot of young cattle ready for market over the next few weeks. And it was vital that they fetched top prices. The survival of the farm itself depended on it. But that meant a huge amount of additional feeding and looking after to keep them in prime condition. Then there was all the other routine work that needed to be done around the farm. But they'd manage, he supposed. They always did. Even if everyone had to work overtime to help out. But of all the luck!

He thought of Joyce and felt a pang of guilt about slipping away from the farm, earlier that evening. She had got back late feeling very stressed. And she had definitely not liked the new man from head office. Reading between the lines from what she'd said, he wasn't exactly over-impressed with her bookkeeping skills either. Steve knew if he stayed, they'd only row. And he couldn't face that. Not tonight. He wondered how the twins were coping. They were great kids. He only wished he could provide more. But there was not much chance of that. Not this year at any rate.

A game of darts was going on in one corner. It was clearly an important match: the men were playing with silent intensity. Steve began to watch. One of the players was a newcomer to the village, and considering he had only been there a couple of months, he was already very popular. Steve didn't like him. He never seemed to be short of money. Perhaps that was why, Steve thought, sourly. But he knew it wasn't just that.

The man's name was Ellis, though whether that was a first name or his surname, no one seemed to know. It was what he called himself. He was heavily built with thick black hair. He made his living as a mechanic and had a growing reputation for repairing broken-down machinery, quickly and cheaply. He was already much in demand from the surrounding farms. Steve had made a point of avoiding him from the start.

He watched Ellis now throw the winning dart and punch the air. Outside, the rain splattered against the little windows like a furtively thrown handful of gravel. Steve drained his pint and put the glass back on the counter. He looked at his watch and considered. 'Just the one, Bill,' he called to the landlord. 'Then I'll be on my way.'

'Don't go tripping over no badgers, Steve!' someone called, and there was a ripple of friendly laughter.

Steve grinned and pushed across a handful of change. He turned and saw Ellis walking towards him, holding empty glasses in both hands. He was taller than Steve by a head and was neatly dressed in a clean T-shirt and new jeans. He wore a pair of combat boots. The type with very big soles.

Steve turned away to avoid him but it was too late. Ellis gave him a friendly nod and banged the glasses down beside him. 'You're from Stoney Cross Farm, aren't you?' he said. 'Steve Jeferson? Am I right? Pleased to meet you. Ellis is the name. Seen you here enough times. Surprised we've not met before this.' And he stuck out his hand.

Steve took it and nearly gasped out loud. The man's grip was crushing. Steve met it with an effort and tried to look unconcerned. Ellis smiled. Steve looked down and saw the scar on the man's outstretched arm. It looked like an old wound. A bite, even. The tissue gleamed white and hard amongst the hair. It must have hurt like hell, Steve thought. And wondered how he'd got it.

'Got any work for me, then?' Ellis asked with a broad grin. 'You farmers always need something done.'

Steve's eyes widened. The cheek of the man! Ellis waited, still smiling. Steve reached for his beer and took a pull at it to cover his annoyance. He wiped the back of his hand across his mouth. 'Maybe,' he said, warily. Then added grudgingly, 'Brakes on the trailer need looking at sometime.'

'I'll give you a call then,' Ellis told him, bringing out his wallet. 'In a week or two? Make a date.' He peeled off a note and passed it across the counter. 'Heard about your badger trouble,' he said, as he picked up two of the refilled glasses.

Steve stared at him, genuinely puzzled.

'Badger trouble! What badger trouble?' He thought for a moment then laughed. 'You shouldn't listen to what they tell you in here, you know. Besides, it only took a few apples. Didn't go anywhere near the hen-house.'

Ellis shrugged. 'I was over your way the other day. Get a lot of badgers out there, do you? Must be quite a few setts up in those woods.'

Steve wondered if the man was just making polite conversation. 'Can't say I've ever noticed.'

'Damn things,' Ellis continued. 'Spreading TB through people's herds. You got cattle, ain't you? Thought I saw some last time I went by.'

Steve nodded. 'Two hundred beef and a bit of arable.' He shrugged. 'But I don't mind the odd badger. Rabbits do far more damage.'

Ellis laughed. 'You're lucky then. That's not what most farmers round here tell me. And all this protected species nonsense.' He bent his head towards Steve. 'Vermin, if you want my opinion,' he said from the side of his mouth.

Steve stared at him in surprise. What was this man's problem? He felt a growing dislike of Ellis. 'Know much about badgers, do you?'

Ellis nodded. His eyes were very dark. It was hard to make out the pupils. 'Enough,' he said. The people at the dartboard were becoming impatient and calling him back. He waved to them. Then put a hand on Steve's arm. 'Seriously,' he said. 'If you ever get any problems with them, you just tell me. Know what I mean?'

He was standing very close. Too close. Almost touching, in fact. Steve could feel the man's body heat. He took a small step backwards. 'No!' he said. 'I don't! Badgers have been around here as long as we have. Live and let live's my motto.' Their eyes locked. 'And I'd get very angry if somebody interfered with any of them, on my land.' Then he smiled back. 'Know what I mean?'

The man stared at him then turned away with a laugh. 'Only joking!' he said. 'No offence! I'll give you a call about that trailer. Next week be all right?'

Steve picked up his beer and drained it in a few large gulps. It tasted flat. The rain met him at the door and by the time he got back to the Land-Rover it was running under the collar of his jacket. It took three attempts before the engine caught and rattled into life. He used his sleeve to clear the inside of the windscreen.

He looked back at the pub. Perhaps he should try the other one in the village. He drove out of the car park, glad to be going home. There was something about that man ... something ... what was that expression he'd heard on the radio? 'Something of the night about him?' 'Yes!' he thought. 'That's him!'

So maybe he'd start taking a walk up through the woods before dark and check on those old setts. There might be a whole lot of new diggings there as well. It wouldn't hurt to keep an eye on things. Just to make sure. Yes! That's what he'd do. And perhaps the twins would come too.

Eight

Steve and Tom were in the hay barn. They had been working there since mid-morning. Tom had lost count of the number of bales they had heaved into the back of the Land-Rover and taken out to the herd. It just seemed endless. His arms and his back ached and standing upright was agony, for the first couple of minutes.

He was covered with dust. It was in his mouth, in his hair and inside his ears. Pieces of hay had slipped down his back and every now and then he had to stop, and scratch frantically. Despite the cold of the afternoon, he was sweating hard.

'Come on, Tom! We've not got all day! Give us some more!'

Tom muttered something under his breath and waved a hand. He dragged the next bale down from the top of the stack. As it landed beside him, he spun it round and flung it on to the floor of the barn, ten metres below. Then he turned and reached for the next one. Each bale weighed close to twenty-five kilos. He had tried to work out how many tons of the stuff he must have moved, but the maths defeated him. So he went back to being a robot again.

It was all Eric's fault. Clumsy plonker! He was always doing stupid things. He had been off work now for the past ten days and this was the second weekend on the trot that Tom had had to work. Sarah hadn't been much use. First of all, she had been helping Joyce get her invoices and things in order. Now, she had a cold coming on. He looked down and saw the strain on Steve's face. Poor old Dad! It had to be worse for him. But all the same, if Eric was going to be laid up for another couple of weeks as his mother reckoned, then his own life was going to be the pits!

He worked mechanically until he heard Steve eventually shout, 'Three more should do us!' He threw the last one down and slid wearily after it. At the bottom, he slumped against a bale and closed his eyes.

'Like some tea?' Steve called. 'There's a bit left.'

Tom didn't bother to reply. He thought he heard his father talking to Buster but didn't care any more. He just wanted to sleep. The next moment, Buster had landed in his lap and was covering his face with hot, wet licks. Protesting loudly, Tom grabbed him and the two of them rolled over on the ground.

Buster was his father's dog. He was a nondescript, ginger-haired mongrel with spindly legs and a laughing face. There was a lot of terrier about him. Quite a bit of whippet too and a lot of other things. He was a stray who had turned up one day outside the kitchen door.

Steve had originally wanted to call him 'Heinz' after the sauce company's famous 57 varieties. But Tom had suggested 'Buster' and the name had stuck. He was full of energy and what he lacked in looks he more than made up for in enthusiasm. He was six years old and went everywhere with Steve.

Tom pushed him away and clambered up, feeling cheered. 'I'll have that tea now,' he said. They stood together sipping it in turns. Steve yawned and rubbed his eyes. He stretched and quickly put a hand on his back, grimacing. Tom remembered the bad time he had had over New Year with it. 'You all right, Dad?'

Steve looked unhappy but shook his head in denial. 'Nothing! Just a twinge.'

Tom handed him the cup. 'Mum says farming's a mug's game.'

Steve did not reply. Instead, he finished off the tea, hurt by what the boy had said. Then he shrugged. 'Your mum's probably right. She usually is. Still . . . if it's in the blood . . . you've got to give it a go.' He put a large hand on Tom's shoulder. 'Depends what's important to you.' Then he smiled. 'Come on then! One more trip to the top meadow should do us!'

Ten minutes later, they were bumping across

the field towards a group of cows. Buster sat between them, his long pink tongue hanging out of the side of his mouth. He looked very pleased with himself. When they reached the cows, they stopped and began to pull out the bales. They scattered hay in deep piles across the field while the cows jostled each other and bent their heads to feed. Their breath steamed upwards from dripping nostrils.

'Good!' said Steve, studying them intently. 'They look all right, don't they? No sign of any weight loss. Thanks, Tom!' he said cheerfully. 'That would have taken me all night.' He walked over to a nearby water trough and banged at the ice with his boot. 'That's better! It's starting to melt. Weather must be changing.'

'Can we go home?' Tom asked. 'Mum'll be back by now.'

Steve looked at his watch. 'Not yet she won't. Suppertime, more like. That's what she's intending. There's this audit thing of hers next week. So today's all overtime for her.'

They lifted the tailboard and secured it in

place with two long steel pins. Back in the cab, Steve hesitated and looked over at Tom.

'What's up?' Tom asked, rubbing Buster's head.

Steve peered at the sky and made a face. 'It'll be dark in an hour . . . I wonder?' He drummed his fingers on top of the steering wheel.

'Come on, Dad. Give!'

Steve hesitated, 'Well . . . it's just something I meant to do weeks ago but what with Eric and everything, there's not been the time.'

Tom nodded. 'So?'

'That old badger sett in the woods. I said I'd take a look. Remember?'

Tom nodded again. 'You think the badger that took the apples lives there?'

Steve considered. 'Might do. But it wasn't that so much. It was something someone said about badgers in the pub. I just got a bad feeling about the guy I was talking to. That's all. I sort of warned him off going up there.'

'You mean he's going to harm them?'

'Who knows? I don't mind badgers but there's lots who don't. And worse!' He switched on the ignition. 'Don't worry. I expect it's nothing. And you've done enough for today. Let's get home and see how Sarah is—'

'Hang on, Dad!' Tom interrupted. 'I don't mind. Honest. Let's take a look.'

Steve grinned. 'Great! Thanks, Tom!' he called, above the noise of the engine.

They drove to the foot of the hill. 'It's a bit of a climb but it won't take that long,' Steve promised. 'Best leave Buster inside.'

They were panting hard by the time they reached the top. 'It used to be round here somewhere,' said Steve, when he had got his breath back. He pointed. 'I remember that old tree. Let's try along there.'

Tom shivered and followed him. It was much colder now. Small patches of snow lay under the bushes and inside the tussocks of grass. He wondered if it had been such a good idea after all. A holly tree bristled red in front of them. Carefully, Steve skirted it then stumbled. 'Brambles!' he called over his shoulder. 'Watch out for them. They're really thick here.'

They pushed through a patch of small fir

trees where the branches whipped at their faces. Then, in front of them, they saw a large patch of open ground surrounded by trees and undergrowth. At the far end, there was a high sandy bank where tree roots stuck out like bony fingers. Tom counted seven large entrances, many times bigger than rabbit holes.

Steve turned and put a finger to his lips. Tom nodded. As quietly as possible, they walked towards the bank, looking around them as they did so. 'See how hard the ground is?' Steve murmured. 'There've been generations of badgers using this place.'

'What for?'

'Everything! They come out here to socialise. They groom each other and play. They even mate out here, as well.'

They stopped at the foot of the bank and gazed up. 'Must be over four metres high,' Tom said. He reached up for the nearest tree root and tugged at it. The wood felt like iron. It was strong enough to swing from.

Steve squatted down in front of one of the entrances. Tom joined him. The tunnel mouth was blackened with use and as smooth as glass at the edges. Tom ran his fingers over them in surprise. 'Feels like marble,' he whispered.

Then he lay full length. The floor of the tunnel was bone dry. He put his head inside and knew he could have got a shoulder in, if he had wanted to. The tunnel ran perfectly straight for a metre, then turned a corner. 'I'll bring a torch, next time I come,' he thought. Outside, he looked at the other tunnels and considered. 'How far back do they go?'

Steve tossed a pebble inside one. 'About a hundred metres. And ones as old as these will have other tunnels criss-crossing on three or four different levels. Like the London Underground.'

'Wow!' said Tom. 'Do you think there're badgers in there now?'

Steve looked round. 'Not sure. No! Can't see any footmarks, or any signs of fresh digging. Can you? But there'll be lots more tunnels like this up here. There's bound to be badgers somewhere.' He looked at the sky. 'Pity the light's going, or we could have had a scout round for old bedding.'

Tom looked puzzled. 'Bedding?'

'It's a dead giveaway. Heaps of old grass and straw. Tells you they've got cubs in there. As soon as the bedding gets dirty, out it goes. They'd probably drag it into those bushes over there. Well away from the sett. They're clean animals, badgers. Not like foxes. If there were foxes here, there'd be old bones and mess scattered everywhere. But there's nothing, is there?'

He stood up. 'Time we were going.'

They walked towards a screen of low bushes. As they reached them, Steve froze in mid-stride and Tom almost bumped into him. Slowly, carefully, Steve indicated. There was a clump of elderberry trees twenty metres in front of them. By now, the daylight was beginning to fade and with every passing minute, the soft blur of dusk grew a little darker.

Tom narrowed his eyes in concentration. He heard Steve catch his breath. And then he too could see it! An unmistakable black and white striped face was staring directly at him. The white stripes almost seemed to glow, they were so vivid. Tom's heart leapt and began hammering with excitement. This was the first live badger he had ever seen.

Cautiously, the badger emerged from the middle of the trees. Tom could just make out the tunnel entrance behind it. Tom thought the badger was almost as big as a fully grown Labrador dog, although it was much lower at the shoulder. It raised its head and slowly tested the air for at least a couple of minutes, then peered round as if searching for any new or strange shapes. Satisfied, it gave a loud grunt and came right out into the open. Tom felt Steve's fingers tighten on his arm.

Behind the badger, three more striped heads followed, almost as large. At first, they stood huddled together, looking round uneasily. Then one of them cuffed another around the head and the two of them began to wrestle, head-butting and growling in mock fury. The third, meanwhile, sat down and began grooming itself.

'That's the old boar!' Steve whispered. 'And the others are yearlings. Last year's cubs. I'll bet there'll be some new cubs somewhere!'

The big male watched for a while then ran towards the yearlings and pushed them apart with his head. All three of them leapt at him and for a while they played together. Eventually, he got to his feet, growling loudly. He shook himself, snarled at one of them and trotted off. Obediently, the others followed, one behind the other.

Tom watched in delight. He had to stop himself calling after them to come back. Seconds later, they disappeared. Steve took a deep breath. 'Well! What d'you think about that, then? I told you you'd like 'em. Didn't I?'

Nine

' 'Bye, Tom!' Sarah grinned and waved her fingers mockingly at him. 'Work hard and get good grades!'

Tom scowled at her, then appealed to his mother standing by the door waiting to go to work. 'Mum! There's nothing wrong with her. She's just skiving off school.'

Joyce Jeferson sighed. They had been over this for the last two mornings. 'Oh come on, Tom!' she chided. 'The doctor said she was to stay home until the end of the week. There's no point her going back until she's fully recovered. That was a nasty thing she had. Be reasonable!'

'So run along, Tom! There's a good boy!'

Sarah told him in a superior voice, grinning all over her face.

'Yes! Come on, Tom!' Mrs Jeferson urged, becoming impatient. 'Why you have to make all this fuss, I can't think.'

'He's the one trying to skive,' Sarah told her. 'He's spent the last few nights hanging round me trying to catch the bug. He wants to get out of his maths project.'

Tom went red. He made a face at her and banged the kitchen door behind them. Sarah watched the car drive down to the road. The track was getting worse, she thought. The potholes were much deeper after all the winter frost and rain.

She washed up the breakfast things then looked round the big farm kitchen with real pleasure. She loved her family but it was wonderful to have the house to herself. Tom was all right as a brother and, being twins, they were naturally close. But he was noisy and soon got bored. It was like having a friendly bull calf around the place. And she had mentally set aside today to catch up on her biology notes.

She was an ambitious and determined girl. A year ago, she had decided she wanted to become a vet. A farm vet, looking after working animals like cows and sheep. Since then, she spent a lot of time chatting with the vet her father used. At first, she had been horrified to learn how many years it took to qualify. And how many exams she would have to pass. But once she had decided it was what she wanted to do, she set to work.

She opened the door now and stepped out into the yard. It was a fine spring morning. The air was warm and the sun felt hot on her face and bare legs. She carried a mug of coffee with her and stood watching the sparrows nest-building in the eaves of a barn. She listened to them scolding each other and squabbling over pieces of straw, while the sun beat down overhead and the cold, damp April ground began to steam.

There was no sign of her father or Buster. Then she remembered him telling her that he would be out most of the day, putting up an electrified cattle fence. She noticed the slurry trailer standing in a corner looking forlorn. There was a man coming some time today to repair the brakes. It had been left out there for him.

Sarah sat at the kitchen table and worked until late morning. Then she yawned loudly and stretched. Time for a break. She put the kettle on and made herself a flu drink. She took an apple from a bowl, picked up a magazine and stepped outside. For a moment she stood with her eyes closed, smiling at the sun. Then she crossed the yard to the hay barn.

The sun streamed in through a large gap in the tiles. The smell of warm grass rose to greet her. Perfect! She pulled a couple of bales together and made herself comfortable. She finished the apple and tossed the core out into the yard. She yawned. She couldn't help it. The flu drink was making her drowsy.

A butterfly landed beside her and she smiled. It was the first one of the year and a real sign that spring was here. It rested with its wings outspread, bathing in the sunlight. After a while, it walked delicately to the edge of a bale and fluttered away. She followed its darting flight upwards but lost it against the brightness of the sky. She yawned again and closed her eyes. Soon she was sinking into a delicious sleep.

Sarah thought she heard her father coming back but was too tired to look. Her eyelids were so heavy. She sank back into a dream. She was running through a wheat field. Now she was ducking down and peering out between the tall stalks. Someone was coming. Someone who must not find her. She crouched down holding her breath.

Something was tickling her nose. She was going to sneeze. Very loudly! She couldn't help it! She woke up with a start and found a man bending over her. A big man with black hair and thick eyebrows. He was holding a piece of straw.

She gave a cry of surprise and pulled away. He put his hand on her shoulder and squatted down. The hand felt very heavy. 'Sorry! Didn't mean to give you a start!' he said, grinning broadly. 'Only you was snoring. I came to see who it was in here. And found a sleeping beauty! Your dad didn't say anything about that!'

Sarah sat up quickly, feeling confused and awkward. She stared at him, not sure what to say. This must be the man who was coming to fix the trailer. She got to her feet, trying to smile. 'It's OK,' she said, at last.

'Sorry if I frightened you!' he called after her. 'I'll get back to that job of your dad's.' There was an old van parked alongside the trailer. She watched him go round to the passenger's side and lift out a bag of tools. He began to whistle.

She felt his eyes following her as she walked back to the house. Inside, she peeked out of a kitchen window. He looked up suddenly and waved and she ducked down, knowing he had seen her. She flamed red with embarrassment and scolded herself for being silly. But she locked the door all the same.

Ten

Marla stood just inside the entrance to the sett, listening intently. The blackbirds were calling to one another, glad the evening was coming. All day long they had flown to and fro from their nest in the elderberry tree, searching for food to satisfy the constant hunger of their four babies. The beauty of their song soared high above the surrounding trees and was lost in the fading sunset. Their work would begin again before dawn the following day. But now, they would soon be settling down to sleep and uncaring of the cries and alarms of the night.

A bumble bee flew into the entrance. Marla snapped at it and missed. It landed on the ground behind her and squeezed into a small hole in the side of the tunnel, buzzing with indignation. She listened to it turning round and round inside its nest, still very angry. Then it too fell silent.

Cautiously, Marla stepped out into the dusk. The air was warm and heavy with scents. Everywhere, sap was rising. A strange yeasty smell that made her want to frisk in delight and roll and wriggle and scratch her back against the stony ground. New life was growing all around her. Tiny green shoots were feathering the branches of the may trees. Blossom swelled inside a million buds, bursting to be free. She gave a snort of pleasure.

She remembered the mud-slide she and Cadoc had made last summer and the fun they had had sliding down it. For a moment, she was tempted to climb to the top of the bank and find it again. Behind her, she heard a cub whimper and she turned to see them all standing there. She barked in irritation and their little striped faces disappeared.

The cubs were six weeks old now and the size of large puppies. But it would be another four weeks at least before she would allow them out of the sett. Until then, they were easy prey for any large predator.

The sight of them brought her back to reality. The ground all round her was dry. She scratched at it to make sure. It was the first time it had been so in days. It had rained heavily for most of the past week so there had been no point going out to find bedding.

But now, the sun had dried the sodden piles of leaves and the bracken and grasses she would need. She wondered what to do first. Should she go off and feed or should she clean out the nursery? The cubs were still delicate and vulnerable to the cold. Without dry bedding, a sudden frost could kill them. And that decided her.

She trotted back inside, fretting now in case the rain should start again before she had had time to drag in the new bedding. She chased the cubs out of the nursery, nipping at their back legs to hurry them. She waited for a moment, listening to their excited little barks fading away. Then she began work.

One of the tunnels close to the nursery was already choked with dirty bedding. She raked up the old grass with her long front claws and gathered it into a large bundle. She arched her back and pushed the heap under her. Then, keeping her chest pressed to the ground, she moved backwards, using her hind quarters to ram the bundle out of the entrance. Once outside, she pushed it a further five metres into the undergrowth, well clear of the sett.

She did this half a dozen times until it had all been removed. She did a final tidying-up inside the entrance, then, satisfied, she set off down the slope towards the fields at the bottom of the hill.

A few hours earlier, Steve Jeferson had moved some cows and their newborn calves into the top field. Marla, standing inside cover at the edge of the wood, caught the smell of fresh hay and, after a moment's hesitation, hurried towards it. The cows' heads turned and followed her as she ran past but they made no attempt to get up. They watched her tug out great mouthfuls and gather them together into a heap.

She hugged the pile to her chest, using her chin and front paws to hold it firmly in place. Then she began to shuffle backwards, sliding along on her elbows and moving surprisingly quickly. Every now and then she looked behind to check her progress. Still going backwards, she climbed the hill and entered the sett.

She spread the hay across the nursery floor before plumping it up into a thick biscuit shape. She made five such journeys before she was satisfied. By then, it was time to feed. She whistled loudly to tell the cubs to wait inside until she returned. Then she ran across the open ground into the woods beyond.

The cubs heard the whistle and listened to her footfalls dying away. They stared at each other, bright-eyed with excitement. They were on their own. The female cub stretched out a paw and tapped the larger male cub smartly on the nose. The male crouched and snarled at her.

She did it again and this time he hurled

himself at her. They rolled over and over in a spitting, kicking, snarling ball, fighting happily. The runt watched and made little darts towards them, leaping backwards whenever they threatened to roll on top of him. He growled at them and occasionally seized a leg or an ear to worry. Eventually, they all arrived back at the entrance.

By now, it was pitch-dark outside. All three of them squeezed together and craned their heads to smell and listen to the night. They gazed in breathless wonder. A trickle of sand started to fall in front of them. The female cub put out a paw and tried to catch it. It grew thicker. Pebbles began to slip down on one side of the entrance.

A vole shot past, chittering to itself in worry. Belatedly, it caught the badgers' scent and spun round, squeaking loudly at the sight of the cubs. They heard its claws scraping at the ground as it ran and craned their necks to see more.

There was an explosive bang and the air was suddenly full of beating wings and bright yellow talons. A long, curved beak stabbed at the vole and the cubs shrank away, hissing in shock. For a split second, the owl was distracted and the vole dodged away, screaming hysterically. It ran between the owl's feet and slipped. The beak thudded down a millimetre from it in a splatter of small stones.

The male cub spat at the owl, then shrank back as two huge eyes glared at him. The vole scurried towards the sett, its mouth wide open. A clawed foot reached out and skewered it to the ground. The owl flew up to its favourite branch. It tore the vole open with a single rip of its beak and swallowed it, head first.

The cubs stared up at the tree and shivered. Wide-eyed, they watched the owl shake out its feathers, launch itself from the branch and come floating towards them. They shrank back and held their breath until the thing was past. To cover their fear, they began to groom each other, but they soon grew bored with this and played hide and seek instead. Some time later, they found a tunnel they had not seen before. It was two levels below their own nursery and the entrance was hidden away beside a large boulder.

Intrigued, they stared at it and took it in turns to peep into the blackness and listen. They bunched together, their noses touching, willing each other on. Their fear and excitement grew rapidly until the two larger cubs began struggling to push past each other. The heavier male cub won, forcing his way past his sister. The runt scampered after them, his heart beating wildly.

Noiselessly, they ran along the tunnel, scampering under tree roots and over stones and always going deeper into the earth. They came across a new scent. An unpleasant smell that grew stronger and made them wrinkle their noses. A female stoat had been along here some hours earlier. She had brought a kill and eaten it. Then she had squatted and marked the ground. The smell of her urine was still fierce and the cubs pressed up against the sides of the tunnel to avoid it.

They had never seen a stoat before and knew nothing of its ferocity. But they instinctively sensed something of its menace. They thought of the owl and even more of their high spirits deserted them. The nursery suddenly seemed a very long way away. They started to jostle and barge one another until they had forgotten all about it. Then the female cub gave a cry of triumph and slipped past. The others followed, hot on her heels, not wanting to be left behind. The smell still followed them.

The tunnel became steeper. Ten metres further on, they heard a strange sound that made them pause. It sounded like the distant sighing of the wind. Their immediate thought was that it was coming towards them, so they backed away. But nothing happened. The noise never varied. It rose and then it fell. Their courage growing, they walked slowly towards it.

The sound grew louder. It was not unfriendly, just strange. It filled the passageway, dominating them. And then they all realized what it was. Something was breathing! A huge animal was sleeping somewhere very close! Perhaps around the next bend!

They stood at the entrance to his sleeping chamber and gazed wide-eyed. Cadoc lay on his stomach, the broad white stripes on his muzzle facing them. His scent filled their nostrils. They recognized it immediately.

They took a step closer and then another. They fluffed up their fur to make themselves look bigger. One of them sneezed and Cadoc leapt to his feet, towering over them, jaws wide open in a snarl.

The cubs were petrified. The hair around their necks stood on end. None of them dared breathe. Still full of sleep, Cadoc stared at them. The larger male cub bared his teeth in defiance and for a moment they all held their ground. Then, as one, they turned and ran, crying for their mother with baby grunts of terror.

Eleven

The telephone rang beside the man's pillow. Its cheerful jingle dragged him reluctantly out of the dream he was enjoying. As his hand groped for the mobile, he peered at the alarm clock. And swore. Who was calling him at this hour of the morning? For Pete's sake!

He propped himself up on an elbow and said, 'Yeah?'

A familiar voice gave the security challenge. He gave the reply and began to wake up in a hurry.

'I know it's early but I've got a lot on,' the caller said gruffly. The man cleared his throat and waited. The other continued. 'Got some new customers. Nice boys. From Yorkshire.

Very keen to see what we can offer. And loaded!' He paused to let the words sink in. 'Money no problem.'

The man frowned. 'You sure they're clean?' he demanded. 'Not undercover cops or ruddy journalists?'

'They've been checked out and they're OK,' the caller reassured. 'Don't you worry about that. That's all been taken care of.' He sounded impatient. 'I was wondering when we could give 'em some sport.'

'When was you thinking of?'

'Three weeks' time. End of the month, say?' His voice became more friendly. 'That new place you found is great. All the punters liked it. Good feedback.'

The man smiled and nodded to himself. 'So how many furry friends do you want?'

There was a pause. 'Can you do three?' The caller continued, ignoring the man's protests. 'I'll pay you four hundred and fifty each.'

'Six! Don't forget, there's old Jimmy too. He'll want fifty pounds a head minimum!'

'I'll pay you five hundred on the nose and

not a penny more. You can settle up with the old man as you want.'

'It's going to be tough getting three,' the man grumbled. 'Then there's all the security and the looking after and things.'

'That's what I'm paying you for. Besides, the old man does all the looking after. So don't give me that,' the caller reminded him. 'Oh! One more thing. Some mates of mine are looking for a bit of outdoor sport. I told 'em they could drive through your area. It's just a one-off. That all right?'

There was a long pause. 'Just keep them away from this place. That's all.'

'OK! I hear you. Call you at the weekend.' There was a click and he rang off.

The man lay back on the pillow and began to scratch his stomach. A slow grin spread across his face. 'Not a bad way to start the day,' he reflected. 'Not bad at all.' Whistling cheerfully, he padded downstairs to let the dog out. Then he put the kettle on.

Twelve

Wednesday was the most important day in Steve Jeferson's week. It was the day he took his cattle to market. Tom and Sarah dreaded it. If the animals fetched a good price, everyone could relax. But if they didn't, there would be phone calls the next day to the bank manager and their parents would walk around looking stressed. On this particular Wednesday, Steve had high hopes. People were eating beef again.

At six o'clock that morning, he went into the yard holding a mug of hot, sweet tea. Buster joined him and together they looked over the cows he had selected. There were ten of them, all Herefords. They bunched together at the far end of the pen, watching suspiciously. Steve put his foot on the gate and sipped his tea in silence. The heifers had come on a treat this past month. They should have no problem making top price. The thought cheered him and he hummed a snatch of song.

At six thirty, a battered-looking cattle truck swung into the yard. The name 'Jack Jones' had once been carefully painted on the sides in elaborate flourishes. But now, the blue and red paint had faded and in places bare metal showed through.

The driver gave Steve a friendly wave and began to reverse towards the pen. Steve stood to one side, watching. When the lorry had got close enough, he banged the flat of his hand against the tailboard. 'That'll do!' he shouted.

The engine gave a clatter, coughed a couple of times and fell silent. The driver came round the side, grinning broadly. He stuck out a large hand. 'I could murder a bacon sandwich.'

'I think we can manage that!' Steve told him.

'Morning, Jack! How are you today?' Joyce looked up with a smile and began laying strips of bacon in a large frying pan.

'Can't complain, Mrs J. But the wife had a bad night. Tossing and turning like a child.'

'Well, I hope it's not anything too serious,' she sympathized.

Jack sat down at the old scrubbed table. 'And dreadful wind. Full of it she was!'

Steve chuckled. 'Thought that was your problem.'

'Don't listen to him!' Joyce said. 'He's a fine one. Out most of the night badger watching, or so he says. Just an excuse to spend more time in the pub, if you ask me.' She put a plate down in front of the driver.

'Don't take all the ketchup, Steve!' she warned.

'Twins all right?' Jack asked, some moments later. 'Doing well at school?'

'They've got exams today. Practice ones,' Joyce told him.

Jack bent over his sandwich. 'Same as mine. Never had all these exams in my day. Well, not that I can remember, any road.'

'Well they do now,' Steve grunted. 'In spades.'

'Trouble is, it's me who worries about the results. Much more than they seem to,' Joyce said, with a little shake of her head.

Steve scowled. 'You've got enough on your plate with your job and everything. So don't get all fussed over some school tests.' He frowned at her. 'The twins are going to be OK. It's us poor devils we should be worrying about.'

The two men munched in silence for a while. 'Right then!' Steve licked his fingers. 'Let's get these beasts loaded!'

The tailboard fell with a crash. The heifers started in fright and backed away. Steve opened the gate and went into the pen whistling cheerfully. He rapped the nearest one on the rump with a long stick and guided it towards the waiting lorry. Once she was inside, the others followed up the ramp without any trouble.

'Tell the twins, "Good luck!" ' Steve called to Joyce, who stood in the kitchen doorway, watching them. Buster sat beside her, whining unhappily. The lorry started up in a cloud of smoke, then slowly juddered its way out of the yard and down the narrow track. Jack clashed the gears as they swung out on to the road. Moments later, they disappeared from sight.

Joyce went inside. She looked at the clock and gave a sigh. Time to get ready for work. And that new manager was coming over in the afternoon with his little sarcasms and superior ways. She went to the foot of the stairs and shouted, 'Tom! Sarah! You're going to be late!'

It was a fifteen-mile drive to market along winding roads and up and down steep-sided hills. Steve skimmed through a newspaper and made casual conversation. When they reached the town they joined a long tailback of other vehicles and crawled along at walking pace. They waited a further half hour before they were allotted stalls to offload the animals into.

The market was crowded. Standing in a queue outside the auctioneer's office, Steve decided it was the busiest day he could remember in years. It was like the old times before the last foot and mouth crisis. 'Can't see your animals being sold till the afternoon, Mr Jeferson,' the auctioneer told him.

He was right. It was late in the day by the time they finally got away. Tired but very cheerful, they drove home. Steve's heifers had fetched good money and he was elated. He was still mentally valuing the rest of the herd, and imagining what he'd be telling the bank manager, when there was a sudden loud clunk from the engine. The next moment, the cab was full of acrid-smelling smoke and the engine stalled.

'Ruddy electrics!' Jack shouted and yanked at the handbrake. He flung open his door and jumped down.

Steve looked around him and swore silently. What a place to break down! They were in the middle of a bleak stretch of moorland, miles from anywhere. On a minor road bordered by sagging barbed-wire fences and pools of brooding water. An old stone wall stretched upwards to a bare hilltop. He took a deep breath to cover his annoyance and clambered out.

A couple of sheep stared at him and moved

away, bleating loudly. He didn't blame them for laughing. After the warmth of the cab, it felt cold. He looked round and sniffed. It would be dark in an hour and the thought depressed him even more.

He had been looking forward to a good supper and an early night. For a moment he toyed with the idea of calling his wife, but decided against it. He knew she'd insist on coming to pick him up, and he couldn't leave Jack out here on his own. These things happened.

Jack came round to join him, wiping his hands on a piece of rag. 'Dynamo's gone,' he announced. 'Burnt out! It's OK though,' he added, seeing the expression on Steve's face, 'there's a new one back in the workshop. Pass me my mobile. Someone'll fetch it. Won't take long. You'll see!'

'You sure you can fix it out here?' Steve demanded.

Jack nodded. 'Easy enough if you've got the right tools.' He laughed. 'And I've got a bin full of 'em at home.'

Later, they shared a last cup of tea from Jack's vacuum flask. It was tepid and tasted of tannin. Steve put his feet up on the dashboard and closed his eyes. Soon, he began to doze.

He was woken by headlights and the hooting of a horn. Jack whooped with delight. Doors banged. Steve peered at his watch but it was too dark to see. He got out of the cab feeling stiff and cold. His mouth tasted rancid. He guessed it was from all the sugar in the tea. Jack and his son were fussing round the engine. He recognized the boy.

'There's one of those emergency breakdown lamps behind my seat,' Jack called, looking round for him. 'Reckon we should show a light in case a car or something comes along. A couple did go by while you were asleep. Do you mind? It's got a red filter.'

The broken-down lorry took up most of the road. Steve checked the lamp then went to lean against the wall. To his surprise, a vehicle came along almost at once. There was a flash of headlights behind him and the growing thump-thump of a stereo system. He shouted a warning to the others and stood at the side of the road, flashing the lamp on and off. The noise grew louder. It was going fast. Very fast!

He screwed his eyes up into the glare, then flung an arm across his face. He was shouting now at the top of his voice but everything was drowned in the boom of the music. The headlights swayed as the driver jammed on the brakes. There was a smell of burning rubber. Steve dropped the lamp and leapt to one side.

He had a brief glimpse of a 4 × 4 with huge, outsized wheels and a row of searchlights mounted on the cab roof before it slid past, centimetres from him. Seconds later, it was accelerating away, the road ahead brilliantly illuminated. Long after its lights disappeared, they could still hear the thump of the bass.

Slowly, the fractured air flowed back. They looked at each other and shook their heads. 'What the hell was that?' Jack demanded, letting out a deep breath. 'Maniacs! Just maniacs! Did you get a look at the driver?'

Steve shook his head.

'The windows were all blacked out,' Jack's son put in excitedly. 'Wow! Fantastic! Great machine!'

Jack wiped his nose on the back of his hand. 'Big-headed yobs!' he grumbled. 'They could have run one of us over. What do they want round here?'

His son bent down and picked up a spanner. 'Come on, Dad! I've got better things to do than this tonight!'

But it was almost ten o'clock before Jack turned the ignition key and the engine burst into life. By then, tempers were beginning to fray. Still, it was wonderful to be moving again, Steve thought and offered up a silent prayer of thanks. They drove in silence for a mile. Then Jack grinned across at Steve. 'Got a joke for you. Forgot to tell you earlier.'

Jack told a good story, Steve thought, and saw headlights appearing in the valley far below. Casually, he looked down at them. A sudden beam like a searchlight flicked on. And another. Then more. Long fingers of brilliant light began to criss-cross the ground reaching out beyond the headlights. Steve could see bushes and a line of hedgerow quite clearly.

'It's that 4 × 4!' Jack cried. 'It must be!'

'Look! There's another one! Coming to join it!' Steve cried.

They watched the headlights of a second vehicle bobbing and swaying. Then, just like the first, its own searchlights came on. It was like looking down on a floodlit football pitch. Jack braked to a halt. 'Come on! Let's see what they're up to!'

They stood by the roadside, gazing down. 'They've turned that stereo system off,' said Jack. 'That's something.'

'They're on Phil Norman's land,' Steve told him. 'He farms all this side of the valley. Wonder if he knows?'

The two vehicles were moving forward now, their searchlights swinging in a wide arc across the ground in front of them. Jack gave a sudden exclamation and slapped his leg. 'I know what they are! They're lampers! Oh my God! We haven't had them round here in years!'

'Lampers?' asked Steve. 'What d'you mean, lampers!'

'Oh come on, mate! And you a farmer?' Jack scoffed. 'They're after animals, of course. Foxes, badgers . . . Everyone's heard of lampers! Not nice people!'

One of the lights darted off to the side and stayed there. Seconds later, the other lights came swooping round to join it. 'Look! They've got something!' Jack pointed. There was a small dark shape in the middle of the glare. Motionless. Even when the vehicles drove up to it.

'What the hell?' Steve breathed.

'It can't move, see! Lost all its senses in the light!'

Heavy doors were slamming shut. Figures were walking into the light. Men's distorted shapes. Shouts and faint laughter. The hair rose on the back of Steve's neck. He knew now. They were going to kill it. He started forward, outraged. The protest surging up from deep inside. 'Hey! You! Stop that!' he bellowed.

And then there was gunfire. Two distinct

cracks a couple of seconds apart. Not the solid bang of a twelve bore. Something far more sinister.

'God Almighty! They've got handguns!' Jack panicked.

Steve hardly noticed him. He made a megaphone of his hands. 'You there! Get out of it! Now!'

Jack grabbed him by the shoulder and swung him round. 'Don't be a damn fool, man! Come on! Get in!' He pushed past him and ran for his lorry. There was no doubt about what he meant. The lorry was already gathering speed by the time Steve got his door closed. Jack kept snatching glances at the lights. His mouth worked silently.

There was only one thing Steve could think of doing. He reached up for his coat and pulled out the mobile. Jack stared at him in horror. 'What do you think you're doing?'

'What does it look like? I'm calling the police!'

Jack knocked the phone from his hand. It fell on the floor somewhere. Steve swore at him. 'Have you gone mad?'

The truck swayed as they roared round a bend. Jack banged the steering wheel with his fist. 'Listen to me! What's the use of telling the police! They've only got six cars to cover the entire county. You think they're going to come screaming out here just because you've seen something nasty? You're crazy!'

He took a deep breath. 'There's no way I'm getting involved in any of this. Nor should you, if you've got any sense!' His face was suddenly running with sweat. He wiped at it with a shirt sleeve. 'Listen! I've heard of these lampers. And don't tell me you haven't! They're trouble. Big trouble.'

'But that was a pistol back there! A revolver, or something.'

'Steve?' Jack said slowly. 'You can fire me if you want to. But this lorry is my living. It puts the food on the table for me and my family. I don't want the police coming by one day and telling me they've found it burnt out in a ditch! Understand?'

They drove home in silence.

Thirteen

The next morning, Steve Jeferson stood in the kitchen making toast. He had had a bad night, full of disturbing dreams. But at least those phantoms had all shrivelled up in the cold light of early morning. And gone.

No matter how he tried, he could not forget the sound of those two gunshots. What sort of people drove round with guns like that? And they surely didn't just use them to kill helpless animals? He thought of his old friend Jack who had been almost hysterical.

He had known Jack for almost twelve years and would never have believed it possible. The man had been seriously afraid. Terrified, in fact, of mcn hc had never met. IIe obviously knew a lot more about these lampers than he'd let on. Perhaps he'd been involved with them in the past? Or even, more recently? Steve groaned out loud. A little shiver ran across his shoulders. Fear was contagious, he realized.

He heard Buster outside, scratching to come in, and opened the kitchen door, glad of the distraction. Joyce was moving about upstairs. Today was a big day for her. For them all, in fact. She was going for a job interview. If she got it, there'd be more money coming in. Quite a bit more. And a nicer boss for her. Well, he hoped so!

He put the kettle on to make her a cup of coffee. It was going to be a long day and he had a lot of things to consider. By the end of it, he would have to decide about last night. Right now, his eyes felt gritty and the only thing he wanted to do was to go back to bed.

The twins were coming downstairs. Breakfast time, already. 'Hi there! Anyone like a boiled egg?' He looked round. They were both staring at him.

'Is this Mum's idea?'

He looked at Sarah. 'Eh?'

'You don't normally do breakfast.'

'No! True! But she's got that job interview this morning at the building society. I thought I'd help out. Don't forget to wish her luck.'

'Ughh! Cold toast,' said Tom.

'I'll make you some fresh. Now there's cereals and things there so if you don't want eggs, then get on with it.'

They ate in silence, watching him over their spoons. 'You were back late, Dad?' Sarah said.

'After midnight,' Tom nodded. 'I heard you come in.'

'Did you get the lorry fixed?' Sarah quizzed. 'Only Mum wasn't too impressed. Well, not at first. Not until Mrs Jones rang. Dad, why didn't you call? We were really worried.'

'She thought you'd gone to a pub,' said Tom. 'We did too.'

'So I heard,' said Steve, drily. 'Nice family I've got I don't think. Here! Toast!' He poured himself some more tea and sat down with them. 'I wish we had been in a pub.' He paused. This wasn't their problem . . . but . . .

He told them.

They listened in silence. 'So what do I do about it? Pretend it never happened? That's what Jack's going to do. He'll deny seeing anything. That's what he told me.'

They looked at each other, eyebrows raised. 'Lamping,' Sarah nodded. 'Just like they told us. The police say you're to go nowhere near them . . .'

'Not unless you want them coming after you with baseball bats,' put in Tom, with relish.

'. . . But you must report it right away if you see anyone lamping or digging out badger setts . . .'

'Here! Hang on, you two! How come you know so much?'

Tom dropped a piece of toast. Buster snapped it up, gratefully. 'We had a local badger group come to our school last week. They were telling us about it.'

'So is it badgers they're after?' Steve asked.

Sarah nodded. 'The police say ten thousand badgers die on the roads every year and that another ten thousand are deliberately killed by people.'

'We meant to tell you but we forgot because of the exams and things,' Tom explained.

Steve looked disbelieving. 'Ten thousand? Killed on purpose? That can't be right.'

'That's what the badger group told us.'

'Have you reported it, Dad?' Sarah asked. 'Dad!' She sounded shocked when he shook his head. 'You've got to! You must! Or the lampers will get away with it!'

'But what about Jack?'

'That's up to him and his conscience,' she told him.

'Dad!' Tom shook his arm. 'Just think if it was one of our badgers up on the hill!'

'Exactly,' Sarah agreed. 'And how would you feel if the lampers dug out our cubs? If you don't tell the police, you've as good as murdered them yourself.'

'All right! All right! I've got the message!' His chair scraped back. He had heard the bedroom door close. Joyce was on her way down. He leant over the table. 'Not a word about this to your mother. Understand! She's got enough on her plate. Oh, and don't forget to wish her good luck.'

After they had all gone, Steve went into the small, untidy room he used for an office. He rummaged through the drawers until he found the large-scale map he was looking for. He studied it carefully, then picked up the telephone.

Phil Norman answered after the third ring. 'You're lucky to get me,' he said. 'Just finished the milking. What can I do for you?'

Steve told him what he had seen the night before. 'I'm positive it was on your land. Can I go and take a look? See if I can find anything?'

There was a long pause. 'I suppose so,' said the man grudgingly. Then added, 'Badgers, foxes, rabbits! They're a damn nuisance all of them. Can't think why the Almighty made them.' And he slammed the phone down.

'Now for the big one,' Steve thought. He took a deep breath and rang the police station. He was lucky. Pete Clegg, the area sergeant, was in. He listened intently, then said, 'My shift ends at midday. I could meet you out there if you like?'

'Fancy a sandwich here first?' Steve suggested.

'You're on!'

Four hours later he was sitting across the kitchen table from Steve. 'Your kids are quite right,' Clegg told him. 'Badger killing is considered a sport by an awful lot of people. And it's on the increase.'

'Sport?' Steve asked in disbelief. He thought for a moment. 'I know some farmers who kill them because of the TB scare. And the odd keeper, who's worried they'll take his pheasant eggs. But, ten thousand? It's unbelievable.'

'It's a fact.' Clegg stirred his tea. 'The farmers and gamekeepers you mention don't play a big part in any of this.' He gave a humourless smile. 'It's all to do with money these days. Big money. Hundreds of thousands of pounds. Let me tell you how it works. You know how they catch badgers?'

'They put a dog down the sett.'

'A terrier, usually,' Clegg agreed. 'With a tracker collar on. The dog finds the badger. The men dig down and pull the badger out. Now, they can either kill it there and then, or, if they're clever, they'll sell it on alive to the baiters. And they're the people we're after. They organize the fights. They're the boys with the real money.'

'How much does a badger fetch?'

Clegg rubbed his chin. 'Four hundred? Five? It depends how big the operation is. Want me to go on?'

Steve nodded.

Clegg swallowed a mouthful of tea. 'First, the baiters find a safe place to stage the fight. Might be out here in the country or an old building in town. Then they put the word out. People bring their dogs from miles around to fight. They bet on them to win. Or how long the dogs will last for. I've heard stories of ten thousand pounds changing hands in a single night.'

'You mean they put their dogs in against the

badger and bet on the outcome?' Steve said slowly.

'Something like that.'

'But doesn't the badger always win? I mean, badgers are tough animals. Most dogs would run a mile sooner than take one on. They've got a terrible bite. Everyone knows that!'

Clegg stared at his hands. 'Yes! Well! These dogs are specially bred to do the business. And besides, they'll use a crowbar to smash the badger's jaw. Or one of its legs. Just to even things up! But a lot of dogs still get killed.'

Steve felt sick. He stood up abruptly and began to pace up and down. 'And your job is to catch them?'

Clegg laughed. 'If only it were that simple! Truth is, even if we catch them red-handed digging out a badger, the odds are, we still can't arrest them.'

'You're joking! Why not?'

The policeman snorted sarcastically. 'It's still legal to dig out foxes, see? So these people travel round with a dead fox, or bits of it, in the back of their vehicle. Then they can say that's what they were doing all the time. Makes a mockery of the law and us!'

'So who are these people?' Steve demanded angrily.

'Hard men!' Clegg told him. 'You'd know them if you saw them. They're a mafia. And as violent. We've had officers beaten up. Farmers too. A couple of them have had their barns set on fire. They're serious criminals!'

'Psychopaths!' muttered Steve.

'That too!' The policeman nodded.

'So, this thing I saw last night. This lamping. What was all that about?'

Clegg considered. 'If you shine a bright light at an animal at night-time, it freezes. It totally paralyses their senses. You've seen a rabbit in a car's headlights? Well, badgers are the same. They just can't move.'

'And then they kill them?'

Clegg nodded. 'Yes! They enjoy it. Now, can we go and have a look at this place?'

It was Buster who found the body. They heard his frenzied barking and went to investigate.

Soon they became aware of the greedy hum of blowflies. They scrambled down into a ditch where the nettles grew chest high. It was dark in there and they had to wait until their eyes grew accustomed to the half-light. They dragged the body out, turning their heads away from the angry swarm of insects.

'It's a female,' Clegg told him.

Steve stared at the corpse. 'Poor old thing. She didn't deserve this, did she?' In death, the badger's eyes were half closed and its lips pulled back in a last, despairing snarl.

They pulled it clear and dropped it on a patch of grass. 'You say you heard two shots?' Clegg asked, waving away the flies.

'Two. Yes,' Steve confirmed. 'God! I'd like to get my hands on the people who did this!'

The policeman bent over the body, peering at the black encrusted blood on top of the head. 'They've got a very strong skull, badgers,' he said. 'There's a thick ridge of bone covering it.' He gave a grunt. 'Here's where the bullets entered!' He knelt down and turned the badger over. 'Now let's find the exit holes.'

'Here's one,' he said a few moments later. 'Looks like a low velocity weapon to make a hole as big as that. A .38 perhaps. Now, where's the other one?' He ran his fingertips slowly over the animal's neck and stomach. 'Well, well, well!' He smiled up at Steve. 'I think there's a bullet still in here. Know much about forensic science, do you, Steve? Amazing what they can tell these days. I've got a good friend in our laboratory. I wouldn't be at all surprised if she finds this gun's got a track record. Thank you, Steve! Thank you very much!' He got to his feet. 'I'll get it back to the station. There's a blanket in my car. I'll just go and get it.'

They lifted the body and placed it in the boot of his car. As they shook hands, Clegg hesitated then said, 'Steve, I don't want Phil Norman to know what we've found. I'm sure he's totally innocent but this could get serious. Come to that, I'd tell no one else either. Not if I was you. And I mean, no one!'

Fourteen

It was June. Midsummer. And Marla was beside herself with excitement. She ran to and fro in front of the sett, barking and yelping and barging into the yearlings, who got in her way. It was a high staccato sound that carried a long way through the wood. A hedgehog heard it and curled up in a pile of old leaves. A pair of jays landed in an old fir tree and hopped along the branches to get a better view.

Marla called again. And this time there was an answering bark. A deep, gruff call. Behind her, the yearlings snorted and chattered and fluffed up their fur. The cubs sat motionless, huddling together, unsure what was happening. But sensing its importance.

Marla lay down in front of the sett and started to whine. This time, the newcomer's bark was much nearer. They could hear him running towards them. The jays screamed a warning then Cadoc burst through the bushes at the far end of the sett.

Marla flung herself at him, growling and whickering in delight, welcoming him back to the family. They wrestled each other like dogs, standing chest to chest, biting at each other's mouth with half-open jaws, twisting and turning. As the excitement rose, the play became even more boisterous and soon the badgers were snapping and biting at each other's rump and tail. And just as suddenly, it stopped.

Cadoc licked Marla's face and for the next half an hour the whole family groomed each other. Cadoc stretched himself out in front of the sett, his eyes closed, purring with pleasure. Every now and then he gave a little shiver of delight as Marla scratched his ears with her long claws and cleaned his fur between her teeth. When they had finished, Cadoc sprayed urine over their feet and all the family took their turn musking each other with their own scent. The family was together again.

On the bank above them, three small, striped heads gazed down. The cubs were almost five months old and the size of large cats. They were fully weaned. Soon they would be adults. It was time for them to learn how to forage for themselves. Cadoc's return marked the end of their babyhood. Tonight, the entire family would leave the sett together for the first time.

But before Marla could call them to her, there was a loud yelp and two cubs came tumbling down the bank in a squirming, biting ball. They collided with Cadoc's back and rolled apart. The next instant, they were on their feet, scrambling over the boar, still screaming.

As the runt came leaping down to join in, they turned on him. The male cub seized him by the ear. There was a sharp yip of pain and they clung together, biting furiously. The female cub raced up the bank, turned and launched herself, knocking them both over.

One of the yearlings tried to join in but the cubs promptly rolled on to their backs, baring their sharp little teeth and snapping at his legs.

Cadoc sat up and smelt the air. It was heavy with the scents of summer. A small breeze was rustling through the tops of the trees. It was time to eat. He got to his feet and shook himself. The cubs stopped their play and watched, and the rest of the family crowded round Cadoc. They rubbed heads and butted each other, impatient to be off. Marla called the cubs to her and they came at once.

Cadoc gave a grunt and led the family through the tangle of bushes and out into the wood. They followed obediently in a ragged line. It was a good night for foraging. The ground was warm and the day's scents rose all round them. Cadoc stopped beside a patch of open ground and cast around.

A weasel had been here some hours earlier. It had caught a vole and eaten it. Cadoc found the place and licked at it. But there was only a sliver of bone left and the distant taste of blood.

A squirrel heard them coming and dropped the pine nut she was carrying. She ran in long bounds to the nearest tree and scolded them as they passed underneath. The cubs looked up and saw a tail twitching and little eyes staring down at them, bright with anger. One of the yearlings found the nut and ate it.

The sounds of the wood grew louder. Trees creaked and shook out their leaves as the air cooled. A hundred strange animals filled the night with their squeakings and murmurs. The fur round the cub's necks fluffed up and they moved closer together. And then the moon broke clear of a bank of cloud and the night was transformed.

Huge oaks reared up in front of them, black and hard in silhouette against the ghostly light. The cubs had never seen trees as big as this before. A moth fluttered into the runt's face. He snapped at it and chased after it. The moth flew upwards into the brightness and the cub sat on his heels, craning his neck to follow its path. Higher and higher it spiralled until it became a flicker of silver in the topmost branches. And then he overbalanced. Luckily, none of the others had seen him. He picked himself up and ran after the family.

The cubs soon realized that this was not a time for playing. They had tried to at first, squabbling amongst themselves and running alongside the yearlings, biting at their ears. But Cadoc had turned and snarled at them. Frightened, they hid behind Marla for protection.

They also noticed that the family kept their noses close to the ground and only rarely looked up. The cubs began to do the same and soon found scent marks they recognized. The unmistakable family identity they all shared. With growing interest, they followed the well-worn trail to the feeding grounds.

Cadoc led them down the hill towards 'Twenty Acre' field. Steve Jeferson had harvested the winter wheat months ago. In its place, he had planted a crop the badgers liked even more. Oats! As they approached, an eddy of wind rippled through the field. Ripe seeds rattled inside the dry husks and the smell of warm oats was overpowering. The badgers broke into a run.

Marla pushed through the first few rows of stalks which the rabbits had already stripped and called the cubs to join her. She pulled the oats to her with a swipe of a paw. Greedily, she ran her teeth along the husks, popping out the seeds and gathering them on her tongue. The cubs tried to copy her but lacked the reach. It was very frustrating until they discovered they could bite through the stalks and trample the husks underfoot.

After a while, Cadoc left the family and lumbered off on his own. It was time to patrol his territory. He stopped and examined all the boundary markers and took great care to spray them with fresh scent. A patch of wild strawberries delayed him for a while, then he resumed his patrol.

He reached the wooden stile that marked the boundary between his area and Findar's. He stood motionless for a while, absorbing the information contained there. But the distinctive scent he was searching for was fading. Other animals had been here earlier that day. A dog, for one. But there was no sign of Findar. No indication that the old boar had been here in the recent past.

Puzzled, he examined the grass all around. Then, very cautiously, he crossed into Findar's territory and began quartering the ground. He stopped every few seconds to listen. Cadoc looked across the field towards the darker shadow of a copse. He knew Findar's sett was in there. Over the past few months, he had often heard the sound of cubs playing and his mate calling to them.

He hesitated, reluctant to invade further. Findar's territory was of no interest to him as such. Even if the boar had abandoned the sett, Cadoc had no territorial interest in acquiring it. Not when his own area was able to support the family. Yet for some reason, he felt uneasy.

Later that night, he slept for an hour under a bush. When he awoke, the eastern sky was already light and the air was expectant. Sunrise was not long off. Grumbling to himself for being out so late, he hurried back to the stile. But there was still no sign of Findar.

As he turned away, he saw a wasp fly out of a hole in a low bank. He stopped to watch. Seconds later, another wasp appeared, then four more. Cadoc's eyes gleamed. His coat bristled with anticipation. He studied the hole for a minute longer then climbed up on top of the bank. The wasps were starting to fly out now in a steady stream. Cadoc waited no longer.

He began to dig, his front claws ripping at the soil like a flail. Sheets of earth sprayed out behind him. In a matter of seconds, his snout was deep inside the ground, just above the spot where the nest was.

Too late, the wasps realized the danger. They attacked in a furious swarm, their bodies bent with rage, stings erect, crawling over his back and shoulders, hopelessly looking for somewhere to sting. Defeated by the thickness of his coat. But by then, Cadoc's long claws were lifting out the delicate, papery nest and he was scrunching up the hundreds of plump grubs inside.

Yawning loudly, he made his way back to the sett, licking his lips in satisfaction. The wasps had given up the pursuit a long time ago and were circling the empty hole in despair. The sun was well above the horizon and the wood was flooded with blinding shafts of light. As he reached the sett, the sun shone directly into his eyes. He snorted, turned his head away and failed to see the figure of the man standing in deep shadow, ten metres away.

Cadoc slipped inside the entrance and hurried along the passage back to his old chamber. Marla was already there. Grunting contentedly, he lay down beside her and they fell asleep, back to back like dogs.

Fifteen

Tom was bored. It was Saturday morning. The first weekend in July and there was nothing to do. It had been a useless summer, so far. It had rained most of the time and now they weren't even going away for a holiday. The Jefersons usually went to Devon for a week. But not this year. There had been a foot and mouth scare at a farm a few miles away and, although it had been a false alarm, his parents had cancelled the booking. 'Just in case.'

But he and Sarah knew it was an excuse, of course. The real reason was that they couldn't afford it. So why didn't their parents come out and say so? He and Sarah weren't stupid. And they didn't deserve to be treated like kids.

Instead, their parents got crosser and crosser with each other. And when they weren't arguing, they took it out on him! If only Mum had got that job, Tom thought bitterly. She'd been on the shortlist too.

He found an opened packet of biscuits in the larder and slipped some out. He couldn't find anything else he liked. Only cheese. He nibbled at them, to make them last as long as possible.

The kitchen clock ticked loudly. It would be hours before his parents returned. They did a weekly shopping trip to the supermarket in the town. Not so long ago, he used to go in with them and meet his friends. Sometimes, Sarah came too. He would get the bus back and be home in time for supper. Then the bus company cancelled the service. Tom had tried cycling there and back but it had not been a success. A thirty-mile round trip took most of the fun out of seeing his schoolmates, but at least he hadn't felt as lonely as he felt now.

He went upstairs and looked in at his sister's

room. As usual, she was reading. 'Want to do something?' he asked.

She looked up and frowned. 'Like what?'

'Get the bikes out?'

She thought about it. 'Where do you want to go?'

'I don't know. Just out.'

She shook her head. 'It's going to rain.'

'Well, do you want to go and look at the badgers?' he persisted.

'Come on, Tom! They'll be asleep. There's nothing to see.'

He went out to the shed where they kept the bikes and rode moodily down to the road. Which way? Did it matter? He cycled automatically, casually noting the miles ticking away on the speedo. Three miles . . . four . . . five. A truck horn blared. He heard the whoosh of air-brakes and a huge, silver-sided container truck roared past.

He clung to the handlebars as the slipstream buffeted him. He wobbled badly and for an awful moment thought he was going to fall under the rear axles. The horn sounded again and he caught sight of the driver's scowling face in the long wing mirror.

A stream of cars started to overtake him. He saw a small side road to his left, almost hidden by a clump of cow parsley, and swung off on to it, praying there'd be nothing coming. He was lucky. The road was clear. He took a deep breath and spat the dust out of his mouth.

The road narrowed. Soon a strip of grass appeared growing up the middle. It began to climb and he changed gear several times. A cold breeze had started to blow, turning the leaves on the trees upside down. Tom shivered and rubbed his arms. A raindrop hit him on the side of the face. Then another. Heavy black clouds were spreading across the sky in front of him.

He saw a huddle of buildings some way ahead, then lost sight of them behind a clump of trees. The wind strengthened, bringing more rain with it. It began to blow straight into his eyes.

He looked away and spotted a high link-fence running parallel to the road. It had obviously been there for some time. Bushes and small trees had forced their way through. In some places, rusting strands of barbed-wire still ran along the top between concrete posts. He rode alongside it for a couple more minutes, then saw the buildings again. And the track leading to them.

He looked behind him, saw the road was empty and turned off. Soon, he was bumping over what was left of a tarmac road. He stopped at the first building he came to and pushed his bike inside. The room was small and dank and smelt of decay. Grey light seeped in through a broken window. Tom sniffed and rubbed the rain from his face. Then he stood in the doorway and looked around.

It must have been an old airfield, he decided. Something like that. There were six identical brick buildings on either side of the road he had come along. And a much bigger one at the far end, with a flight of wooden steps running up the outside.

There was a large oil stain on the ground in front of him. He watched the bright patterns of red and yellow and blue swirl and flow in the rain. There was another patch further along and he wondered why anyone should want to come out here. Courting couples, maybe? He turned back inside and saw a cigarette packet lying beside the door. He moved it with his foot. It had been dropped quite recently. The paper inside still looked dry.

The rain was easing. He waited another five minutes and went outside. He walked between the buildings, looking inside each one as he passed. There were a lot more oil patches. He reached the two-storey building and guessed it must have been the old control tower. The deduction pleased him. He decided to explore.

He paused at the foot of the stairs and looked up. The steps looked solid enough, he thought. He even counted three that had been replaced recently. The wood was new. That struck him as odd. He banged his foot down hard on the first step to see if it would take his weight. It was solid. He did the same on the next two. He seized hold of the handrail and shook it. It was firm.

Intrigued, he climbed the stairs. But the room was depressing. The windows were all broken. Pieces of glass lay along the floor, underneath. There were patches of fungus on all the walls. There were also cigarette butts and two crushed plastic cups. And again, Tom wondered why anyone should want to come up here. There wasn't even anything to sit on.

The view was good, though. A wide expanse of flat, weed-covered ground stretched away on all sides. He could see where the aircraft hangars had been and their dispersal bays. He wondered what sort of aircraft had taken off from here. His father would know. Away in the distance, he could see parts of the perimeter fence and even the gate he had come in by. He decided some model aircraft club or other must use the place. That would make sense. He stayed there for a few minutes longer, then left.

The stairs were more slippery going down, so he took his time. When he reached the ground, he noticed another door to the building. He'd just take a quick look inside.

The door opened easily and he stood on the threshold, waiting for his eyes to adjust to the gloom.

There was a strong smell of urine and he wrinkled his nose. He began to walk down a long corridor, peering into each of the rooms. In one of them, a startled bird looked at him from a window ledge and flew off, shrilling in alarm. The sound died away and the silence closed back over him.

There were still a few faded signs on the walls and in one of the rooms he saw a battered filing cabinet. He tugged open the drawers but found nothing. Looking out, he saw the rain had started again. There were two more doors ahead of him, both closed. The smell was getting worse. He kicked at the very end one and it flew open with a bang. Tom jumped back. Inside, stood an old lavatory with no seat. Wads of newspaper blocked the bowl. A dead fly lay on its back in the stained water. Tom grimaced.

Now, there was only the one room left. But he had seen enough. Time to go. As he was turning away, something made him stop and look again. It took him a second or so to realize what it was. The door was as battered as all the others. But it had a handle. A proper handle with a keyhole underneath. It was new and shiny.

Someone must have fitted it, not very long ago. But why? What was that! He spun round, staring up the corridor. And slowly breathed out in relief. Just his imagination. All the same, this was just the sort of place a murderer would choose to meet his victim. And hide the body! He licked his lips and listened, ears straining. Total concentration. Rain was pitter-pattering on the weeds outside. Otherwise, there was silence. As if the building was holding its breath.

Tom swallowed. He wanted to get out. To walk away quickly back into the daylight. Instead, his fingers reached for the door handle. He wanted to yank them away. This was mad! He was scaring himself to death. He took a deep breath and grasped the handle properly. He remembered thinking it felt sticky. Then he flung it open.

Nothing happened! No one screamed or came leaping out at him. It was pitch-dark in there. He waited while the silence grew deeper. What was that smell? There was stale tobacco smoke. But it wasn't that. It was another strange, musty scent.

He saw a light switch on the wall beside him and automatically switched it on. The next moment, he was gasping in surprise. Powerful electric lights hung down from the roof, flooding the room in a pool of light. It looked like a boxing ring. Something like that. He stared open-mouthed. Did people come here to fight? It didn't make sense.

He took a bold step inside and peered around. It was a big room with no windows that he could see. There were pieces of straw lying scattered across the floor and lengths of baling twine in one corner. Why would anyone bring bales of straw in here and then take them out again?

The floor in front of him had been swept. He could see brush marks quite clearly and some scuffed footprints, coming towards him.

He stepped back at once. He didn't like this place. There was something wrong about it. He felt like an intruder peeping in at someone's nasty secret.

Tom flicked off the light and pulled the door shut behind him. He wiped his hands on his jeans to clean them. As he did so, he heard the sound of vehicles pulling up outside.

Sixteen

Tom listened in disbelief. This couldn't be happening! Car doors were slamming. He could hear voices. Getting louder. Coming in here! He must hide but his feet were rooted to the spot. He was helpless. Like a rabbit.

He had done nothing wrong. Nothing at all. There had been no 'Keep Out' signs. But, instinctively, he knew that he did not want these people to find him. Or discover who he was. He was afraid. So afraid, he began to shake.

Then his subconscious took over. Adrenalin flooded through his body. Without a second thought, he backed into the filthy lavatory and squeezed behind the door. As he did so, he heard a man's voice at the other end of the corridor. 'Here we are, then!' He sounded very sure of himself. 'Best place we've had in years. Come on in.'

Tom held his breath. Footsteps were thudding down the corridor towards him. How many men were there? Three, four? And then sweat began running down the inside of his arms. What if one of them wanted to come in here?

'This is it!' said the same voice. Tom felt the door pushing against his kneecaps. Someone was leaning against it. He bit the front of his tongue and his mouth filled with pain. As he closed his eyes he heard the click of the light switch. And the first voice saying, 'Not your actual Olympia but not bad, eh?'

'Great!' said a second man. 'Couldn't be better.'

'How did you get the electrics all hooked up?' someone else asked.

They must have all moved inside the room because the first man's voice was muffled. Tom thought he heard him say, 'Never turned it off, did they? This place was supposed to be a young offenders' prison. Then a refugee centre. But they never got round to doing any of it. So I tapped into the mains.' They all laughed.

'Should take thirty punters?' a new voice asked. 'What you reckon?'

'Easy! Come on. I'll show you how the security works.'

One of the men started to cough. Tom could hear the phlegm sucking at the back of his throat. Powerful shoulders pushed at Tom's door. It quivered. Then stuck. A hand came round, gripping the inside of the door, centimetres from the boy's face. The man hawked and spat into the lavatory bowl. Tom had a fleeting glimpse of a bright red T-shirt. As the voices retreated up the corridor, he thought he heard one of them say, 'Tonight, then. Midnight. Happy?' But he couldn't swear to it.

The door at the far end banged. The voices faded. Tom breathed a long, long sigh. But he did not move. He stayed where he was, listening. The men were still close. He guessed they had gone up the stairs to the old viewing platform. They might come back here at any moment. The thought made him shiver. It was an age before he heard engines start up. Two of them. Minutes later, they drove off. Were there any more vehicles out there? He didn't know.

He went on waiting, wondering how long it would all last. In the end, a bursting bladder drove him out. The door screeched as he forced it open. The noise seemed to fill the corridor but there was nothing he could do about it.

He hesitated, resigned to whatever might happen next. But no one came to investigate. The door at the far end remained closed. Next, he slipped into the first room he found with a window and hoisted himself up. A hole had been knocked in the wall opposite and there were bricks and lumps of concrete scattered everywhere. Nettles grew in patches amongst the rubble. Tom swung his legs over and jumped down.

He landed on some loose bricks and went sprawling. He flung out a hand to save himself and lay there, winded. As he pushed himself up, his hand touched something strangely yielding. He jerked it away with a cry of disgust. Whatever it was, it was dead.

He stirred the nettles with his foot. It wasn't a cat or a dog. He shuddered. It was a very small badger. Not much bigger than a cub. A badger with the skull showing white through the torn fur. He stared at it in horror. Then, squatted down and looked more closely at the animal's ripped and mangled body.

His revulsion gave way to anger. This was no accident. The badger had been savaged to death. He was sure of it. And he knew then with certainty, that between this pathetic little body and the men he had heard talking, there was an undeniable connection. He must get out of here. Fast!

Picking his way over the broken ground, he sidled round towards the front of the building. Deliberately, he lay full-length on the ground and carefully squirmed the last couple of metres, to the very edge of the tarmac. He peered round.

There was nothing. No sign of anyone. He took a very deep breath and ran! His bike was where he had left it. Out of the rain. Out of sight. He pedalled furiously, bending low over the handlebars, waiting for the shout of discovery. And he kept looking back over his shoulder until he reached the main road.

Seventeen

Tom flung his bike down beside the kitchen door and burst in. Sarah was sitting at the table, eating. She looked at him in surprise. 'What's wrong?' Then, 'What's happened, Tom? Tell me!'

'I've found the baiters!' he gasped. 'I know where they are!'

'Baiters? What baiters?'

Tom's chest heaved. For a moment, he couldn't speak.

'Oh, come on in!' she cried. 'And close the door. It's cold. And calm down!'

Tom stood over her. 'I found a dead badger. All torn and horrible. And there were men there, as well!'

'Tom! Take it easy! Here, have a glass of water.' She went to the sink. Tom slumped on to her chair and put his head on the table. His shoulders shook.

'It's true, Sarah. Swear to God. There were these men. I hid behind a door.'

'What's all this stuff in your hair? Ugh!' she exclaimed. 'It's cobwebs!'

'There were lots of them behind the door. That's what I'm telling you.' He pushed her hand away. 'Just let me explain, will you! And stop interrupting!'

She listened in growing amazement, piecing it together into a logical whole. At the end of it, she looked grave. 'You promise, you really promise, you're not making any of this up?'

Tom shook his head, wearily. He felt drained now of all emotion.

'But you didn't see their faces?'

'No.' He remembered how it had felt hiding behind the door. 'No way!'

She thought for a moment. 'So we've not got a description to give Dad. That's a pity. What sort of men were they?'

Tom shrugged. 'How do I know? They were big. Strong, I mean. And they seemed in control.'

'And there's something happening there tonight?'

Tom nodded. 'Midnight, one of them said. Least, I think he did.' He wrinkled his brow. 'I'm pretty sure he did.'

'How far away is this airfield?'

'Eight miles. I got back in twenty minutes!'

Sarah peered out of the window. 'It's them! They're back.' She turned to face him. 'Listen, Tom. Just be cool about all this. Get Dad on his own, first. Then tell him. OK?'

Tom nodded.

Her voice softened. 'That was very brave of you, Tom.' They both went outside.

The Jefersons' car jerked to a stop. Buster, who had been standing up in the back, gave a yelp and slid off the seat. The twins saw the strained faces of their parents. 'Oh no!' groaned Sarah. 'They've had another row!'

Joyce Jeferson threw open her door. She gave the twins a quick smile, then busied herself looking for something in her handbag. Sarah saw at once how upset she was. Steve stayed in the driver's seat, looking straight ahead. Tom rapped on the windscreen then went to let Buster out. The little dog greeted him like a long-lost friend.

'Oh come off it!' Sarah heard her mother say. 'I'm not sitting in here all day. Get the boot open!'

'Wait, Tom!' Sarah warned, recognizing the signs. She made a grab for his arm. But Tom was too full of excitement to care.

'Mum! Dad!' he burst out, as they got out of the car. 'I know where the badger baiters are. And I found a dead badger there, so that proves it! And the men are going back there tonight.'

Joyce turned on him. 'I'm sick and tired hearing about badgers!' she shouted. 'Sick and tired! Do you hear? I wish I'd never heard of the things!' She looked at Steve. 'It's your fault for encouraging them!'

'But, Mum! I found this old airfield,' Tom began.

Joyce ignored him and shook her finger at Sarah. 'And I thought I told you, Miss, to keep an eye on him! Fat lot of use you are! Only person you think of is yourself. Now, let's get this shopping inside.'

Sarah was white with anger. 'Mum! That's not fair,' she began.

'It's true, Dad! Honest!' Tom interrupted.

One of the plastic shopping bags fell over. Quick as a flash, Buster seized a packet of sausages and began shaking it. Steve made a grab for them. The dog's teeth sliced through the wrapping and the sausages landed in a puddle. Mrs Jeferson screamed and hit Buster.

Steve swore. 'For God's sake!'

Joyce glared at him. 'Don't you swear at me!'

Steve's face went very red. 'Just do what your mother says!' he said brusquely, and walked away.

They unloaded the car in silence. When everything had been put away, Joyce looked at the twins. 'I don't want to hear the word "badger" again today, from either of you. Do you understand?' She made them look at her.

'And now you can both go to your rooms and start tidying them. I'll come up in half an hour.'

'Sorry,' said Tom, when they were upstairs. 'I messed up, didn't I?'

'You sure did! Nice one . . . I don't think!' But Sarah wasn't really listening to him. She was seething at the unfairness of her mother's remark.

'And Dad's gone off in the Land-Rover somewhere,' Tom told her. 'I heard him go. He won't be back for ages.' He kicked at a book lying on the floor. 'Now we'll never know what those men were up to. For certain, I mean.'

Something in his voice caught her attention. 'You're right!' she said, slowly. 'We won't! Not if Mum and Dad go on like this.'

Tom made a face. 'Will they! They'll be in a mood now for the rest of the day.'

'Well, I'm sick of being treated like a kid. We've spent hours watching those badgers. And now we'll never find out . . . unless . . .'

Tom frowned. 'Unless what?'

'Unless we go and see for ourselves! Like . . .

tonight! Because that's the only way we'll ever really know.' She put her hands on her hips. 'So tell me, Tom, are you up for it?'

Eighteen

Tom switched on his bedside light and looked at the clock again. Almost midnight. He couldn't believe they were doing this. It had seemed a brilliant idea at teatime. Now, he wasn't at all sure. His bed was warm and inviting. Then he thought of the dead badger he had found, and of their own thriving family up on the hill. Sarah was right. They had to find out.

He threw off the duvet and swung his legs out of bed. It was time to get dressed. He had put his clothes on the floor, some hours earlier. Jeans and a black fleece. A few minutes later, he crossed to the window and poked his head out. A solitary light burned in the yard. His father must have forgotten to switch it off when he came in. And the rain had stopped, so that was a bonus.

He picked up his trainers and cautiously opened the bedroom door. The stairs were no problem. He knew which ones creaked. The last thing he needed was to wake his parents. There'd been more than enough upsets already that day. Sarah was waiting for him in the kitchen. She was standing by the back door where the yard light threw her shadow across the tiled floor. 'Didn't think you were coming!' she whispered. Buster sat up in his basket and looked puzzled. Tom bent over the dog and patted him. 'Won't be long. You be a good boy!' They locked the door behind them with the spare key.

Tom looked up at his parents' window. It was in darkness. No one seemed to have heard them leaving. The night air was cold and he thought again of his warm bed and hesitated, knowing it was not too late to go back. Sarah was already pushing her bike down to the road. He hurried after her. The trouble with Sarah, he thought crossly, was that she always took over everything. Moments later, they were pedalling smoothly through the night.

It wasn't easy finding the side road. He was amazed how different everything looked at night. As it was, they very nearly missed it, only spotting it at the last moment in the lights of an overtaking car.

As the little road started to climb, Tom was struck by the emptiness of the country around them. There wasn't a house or streetlight to be seen. It was pitch-black wherever he looked. He couldn't imagine anyone driving along here unless they had a very special reason for coming.

At that precise moment, there was a flash of light behind them. Tom looked back and saw a pair of headlights blazing through the darkness. Seconds later, he heard the sound of a vehicle accelerating and the whine of tyres. He heard Sarah's shout of alarm.

He skidded to a halt looking for somewhere to hide. The road was lined with blackthorn hedges, their spiky branches bristling in warning. But there was a huge old elm ten metres in front of them, half buried in the hedgerow. The glow from the approaching headlights was already reaching out towards them.

'Come on!' he shouted. 'Behind that tree!' He pedalled like a madman, reached the tree and leapt off. Sharp thorns slashed at his hands and face. But there was room behind it. Just! He flung his bike down, turned and grabbed Sarah's. 'Quick! Get in!'

Sarah screwed her eyes shut as the vehicle swept towards them. Moments later, she smelt the heat of the engine as it roared past. Grit stung her face. She lay motionless, waiting for the screech of brakes and the sound of the vehicle reversing. But none came.

She opened her eyes one at a time and saw the taillights gleam red in the distance. The next moment they were gone. Slowly, shakily, they clambered out. Tom sucked the cuts on his hands. 'You sure you want to go on with this?' he asked. 'We may not be so lucky next time.'

Sarah hesitated. 'How much further?'

'Not very far. You turn right at the top of the hill. Where that car went. The airfield's about a mile, along there.'

Fifteen minutes later, they were crouching behind a large bush. Waiting. Another vehicle had turned on to the road and was coming up behind them. It was moving very slowly, as if the driver wasn't too sure where he was going. As it passed, they saw it was a Land-Rover. Someone was leaning out of the passenger window. Tom saw the perimeter fence show up in its headlights and had a fleeting glimpse of a large hole in the wire mesh.

Then the Land-Rover's headlights switched off and it continued on sidelights only. Puzzled, Tom stood up. He saw torches waving further down the road and guessed they were the signals the driver had been looking for. The vehicle braked and turned off the road.

He was just going to step out when there was a loud hiss of static and a man's voice said, 'That's the last one!' Tom froze, too shocked to think. A dark shape detached itself from the background of trees and crossed the road in front of him. He saw the green glow of the mobile and heard the crunch of boots. A man passed three metres away from him.

Tom stared ahead, rigid with disbelief. He waited until the sound of footsteps died away. It seemed to take a very long time. Sarah stood behind him, hardly daring to breathe. Slowly, very slowly, they relaxed. 'That was close! What was he doing?' she hissed.

'A lookout, I suppose. We've got to be really careful now. There're more men along the road, with torches,' he breathed. 'Remember that.'

They left their bicycles beside the bushes and made their way towards the fence. They followed it along to the hole Tom had spotted. When they reached it, they sank down and listened again.

'You sure you want to go on?' he asked.

She said nothing.

'Because if you do, we should get in here.'

Sarah looked at him. And decided. 'We can't go back now. Let's go!'

The fence was rusty and it didn't take them long to bend back the edges and make the gap big enough to squeeze through. As they did so, the moon appeared, low down in the sky. It was not much more than treetop height and threw a sickly light across the ground. But it was enough to see by.

They could just make out the buildings in the general gloom. They were four or five hundred metres away. Tom pointed at them. 'The control tower's the furthest one. See it? That's what we're heading for.' He looked at her. 'Ready?' She gave him a thumbs-up. 'Come on then!' Bending double, he began to run.

They reached the nearest building and crouched down beside it. For a while, neither of them could say anything. They were too busy getting their breath back. Sarah listened to her heart pounding and was secretly thrilled. They had made it. They had got in and no one had seen them. Sweat was running into her eyes, making them sting. She leant her back against the wall and rubbed at them.

Tom was already back on his feet, impatient

to get on. The longer they stayed here, the greater the chance of someone seeing them. Keeping close to the wall, he tiptoed to the end of the building. Carefully, he peered round. And jumped back! A 4 × 4 was parked there. Its tailboard hanging open. Empty. It was so close, he could almost reach out and touch it.

He put a finger to his lips and waited for Sarah to join him. 'There may be men patrolling. If you see any . . . freeze!' Then together, they darted across the gap to the next hut. This time, Sarah cupped a hand over her ear and motioned to him to listen. She was right. He could hear people too.

They made their way along the line of huts, until they reached the back of the control tower itself. Tom remembered his last trip there. The room with the lights hanging down. And the men. On the other side of this wall. He swallowed, nervously.

There was no mistaking the sound of voices now. A rising hum that grew louder by the minute. Laughter too. He wondered how many people there were in there. Twenty? Thirty? He realized with a sinking feeling in his stomach that he didn't want to be here at all. And then they heard snarling! A horrible throaty sound full of menace which made everything seem much worse.

Sarah put her mouth close to his ear. 'Tom! The dogs! Remember what they told us at school?'

She was interrupted by a man's voice shouting from inside. They pressed their heads against the wall to hear better. There was a great roar of triumph that swelled with excitement. A bellow that grew louder and more fierce. Ugly voices full of hate. Yelling for pain and blood. Sarah's skin crawled. There was something terrible happening in there. There was no mistaking it. As they gaped at one another, the dogs became hysterical. Barking and yelping, growling and whimpering until the noise became a continuous assault of pain and despair. And then, even above that hubbub, they heard a loud, splintering crack and an animal screaming.

It was a demented shriek. The cry of an animal in agony. It seemed to last for ever. Sarah clutched at Tom, her face ugly with shock. They shrank away and stared at the wall in horror. Inside, the shouting reached fever pitch. Time stood still. The two of them waited. Unable to move. Paralysed by this terrible discovery of human wickedness. And knowing for the first time in their lives, that they were in the presence of real evil.

But they also knew instinctively that this was neither the time nor place to express their own emotions, no matter how much they wanted to shout and scream and cry. Their very own lives could be in danger. They were out of their depth. This was a time to hide or run away and hope to God the men inside would never find them or know who they were.

And then an engine started, close to them. Tom seized her arm and dragged her down until they were both lying slumped against the wall. It was too late now to run! There was a surge of voices. Men calling to one another. There was laughter. Cheery goodbyes. More engines revving up. There was movement all round them.

Two men came round the side of the control tower and walked towards them. Sarah's fingers found his and began to crush them. She was shaking. A lighter flared. Cigarettes glowed and the smell of smoke drifted towards them.

'That was great!' said a voice. 'The lads really enjoyed it!'

The second man laughed. 'Well, we try and please. You know that!'

Sarah's heart missed several beats. That voice was familiar. She'd heard it before. She knew she had!

Their cigarettes glowed. The same voice went on, 'It's a good place this. Right out in the middle of nowhere.'

'Yeah, but we musn't overdo it. Got to be careful. One more time then we go back to the old quarry.'

'You're the boss,' the second man agreed. 'So when's the next time?'

'You just get me another badger like that last one. All right?'

'Done!' laughed the second man. 'Never let you down yet, have I? Besides, I know just the place. I've had my eye on it for a long time.'

The first man sounded pleased. 'Great. I'll call you later.' He dropped his cigarette and trod on it. 'Well, must be on my way. Got a long drive back.'

The moon climbed higher and bathed the ground in a cold blue light. An owl was calling from nearby. They had heard the door in the control tower slam shut and the last vehicle drive off. It wasn't a dream, Tom thought. Sarah was sitting here next to him and he could feel her body shivering. He put an arm round her shoulders and squeezed.

'I was right, wasn't I?'

She nodded.

He was silent, trying to find the words. 'Do we . . . do we have to . . . go in there and look? Find evidence?'

She shuddered. 'No way!' Awkwardly, she began to get up, and gave a little moan as the pins and needles in her legs found her. 'We know what happened. We heard, didn't we?'

They walked along the tarmac back towards the road. In a doorway, a beer can lay on its side. Tom said quietly, 'One of those men was in the building yesterday. I recognized his voice.'

'Tom!' She turned towards him, her face chalky white in the moonlight. 'I know his name, Tom. I know who it is!'

Nineteen

It was Buster who betrayed them. They had taken great care not to make any noise as they put their bicycles away. But as they entered the kitchen, the dog had sensed their distress. He began to bark. Once, twice, and then continuously. The more they tried to stop him, the louder he barked.

Lights flashed on. Steve Jeferson came thumping down the stairs with an old police truncheon in his hand. Joyce was close behind him. When the two adults saw them, they stood open-mouthed in disbelief. At any other time, the expressions on their faces would have been funny.

Sarah seized the initiative. 'Tom was right.

Those men are badger baiters. We heard everything. It was horrible!' She stared at them defiantly, then her reserve broke and she burst into tears.

Mrs Jeferson rushed across and put her arms around her. Steve looked at Tom intently and saw the stress on the boy's face. He grunted. 'I'll phone Sergeant Clegg first thing in the morning.'

The policeman arrived before breakfast. Steve met him outside and the two men paced up and down the yard for a couple of minutes. Then Steve opened the kitchen door and Clegg strode in, his face red and worried.

Steve followed, looking very serious. He bent over the twins and said quietly, 'Just tell Sergeant Clegg exactly what happened last night. Tell him everything!'

They did.

There was a stunned silence when they had finished. Joyce shook her head in horror and reached for a handkerchief. She blew her nose, noisily, and Sarah knew she was close to tears.

Steve took a deep breath and stared out into the yard.

The policeman sat down heavily. He closed his eyes and groaned out loud. Then he turned on the twins, his voice loud with anger. 'Don't you ever do that again! Ever! Ever!' Sarah stared at him defiantly, then at her parents, who were standing on either side of the policeman. Tom's face flushed with embarrassment.

Sergeant Clegg banged his hand down on the table. 'You were so lucky! You've just no idea! No idea at all! Have you, Tom?' His eyes bored into the boy. 'Do you know what they'd have done if they'd found you?'

Tom went scarlet. He began to mumble something but it was drowned by Clegg's raised voice. 'They'd have given you a good beating for a start. And after that, who knows? These people are sadists. They enjoy watching live animals being torn to pieces.'

'And as for you, Miss.' Clegg turned to Sarah. 'You're as bad as your brother! Everything I've told him applies to you!' The policeman shook his head and marvelled in silence. No one said anything. There was a long pause. Buster went over to the kitchen door and whined to be let out. The kitchen clock went on ticking, loudly.

Clegg gave a sigh and looked up at Steve and Joyce. His voice was back under control. He shook his head. 'But you want to know something? These two young people of yours have given us the best intelligence we've had in years. Frankly, it could be a breakthrough.'

Joyce was taken aback. She looked proudly at the twins and smiled. Steve pulled out a chair for her and she sat down beside Sarah.

'So the kids were right after all?' Steve mused. 'There was baiting going on.'

'No doubt about it,' Clegg agreed and he began to tick off the points on the fingers of his hand. 'First, there's the dead badger Tom found, and the condition it was in. Second, they both heard one of the men ask for "another good badger". Then, there were the lookouts and the security measures they had in place. And lastly, Tom and Sarah heard some of what was happening. The dogs, the shouting and the animal screaming.'

Tom remembered the sound of the bone snapping but said nothing.

'And lastly,' Clegg reminded them, 'Sarah insists she knows who one of the men is. Am I right?'

'It was Ellis. I'm positive!'

Sergeant Clegg looked pleased. 'We've had our eye on Mr Ellis for some time now. But this is the best lead yet.'

Steve touched Joyce's arm. 'Ellis is that new bloke at the garage. He's living at old Mrs White's place.'

Joyce screwed up her face in disbelief. 'You mean the man who came to fix your trailer? That's him! And you let him come here!'

'Well, I didn't know! How was I supposed to know?' Angrily, he turned back to the policeman. 'So what happens next?'

The policeman shrugged. 'Nothing . . . yet.'

They stared at him.

'Nothing? What d'you mean . . . nothing!'

cried Mrs Jeferson. 'Now you know where these baiters are meeting, why can't you watch the airfield and arrest them? You can't do, "Nothing"!'

'They'll be there the next time,' Tom put in. 'And then they're going back to the quarry. That's what they said.'

'So why can't you arrest this Ellis creature?' Joyce insisted.

Sergeant Clegg gave her a rueful smile. 'I wish I could, Mrs Jeferson. But we need hard facts. Proof that will stand up in court. All we've actually got here, I'm afraid, is the unsubstantiated word of a couple of thirteen-year-olds.'

Joyce looked at him in disbelief.

'Look!' Clegg explained. 'It was late at night. Sarah was terrified. She's told us she was. She never even got to see Ellis's face. She "thinks" it was him. But there's no proof. Any half-reasonable defence lawyer would make a laughing stock out of us.'

'But we heard the badger screaming!' cried Tom.

'It was him!' Sarah was suddenly close to tears. 'I swear it was!'

'Why don't we go to the airfield now,' Steve demanded, 'and see if we can find the evidence?'

'Then I can show you the dead badger!' Tom agreed, eagerly.

Clegg shook his head. 'I know you can, Tom. But I can't risk running into Ellis or anyone else who might be out there. That would warn the baiters that we're on to them.'

'Well then, why can't you have the airfield watched?' Joyce demanded. 'You can't just do nothing! I mean . . .' She looked distraught. 'I know the twins were very stupid but they've found you the right place! And that's much more than the police have done!'

Clegg shifted in his chair.

'You haven't got the resources. Is that it?' Steve asked.

The sergeant nodded.

Steve frowned, remembering. 'What about forensic? Remember the lampers and the badger we found shot? What's happened to that?'

'Same thing,' Clegg replied. 'Forensic have been rushed off their feet with normal human crime. They've not had a chance to look at it yet. They will though. I promise you. In fact, I'll call them today.'

'So what are we supposed to do now?' Sarah asked, in a voice quivering with resentment.

Clegg frowned at her. '*You*,' he said, with heavy emphasis, 'will do nothing. And that goes for you, Tom. By all means keep your and eyes open. But leave this to us to sort out!'

He stood up. 'I'm really sorry,' he said. 'But we've got to catch them at it red-handed. Then, we can put them away where they belong! Right now, we've got to find out when their next meet is. If we can discover that, then we'll have them!'

'Well,' said Steve, opening the door for him, 'from now on, I'll be keeping a damn close eye on our sett! I'll check it every day.'

Much later that afternoon, Sarah went into her brother's room. She closed the door behind her. 'Tom!' she said firmly. 'I'm positive it was Ellis. Do you believe me?'

Tom scratched his head. 'Well, yes. I suppose so. If you're really sure.'

She came closer until she was standing beside him. 'I know it was him! I just know it. And if I'm right,' she said, 'I mean, if he is one of the baiters, then he must know everything that's going on.'

Tom shrugged. 'So?'

Sarah looked at him and gave him a slow smile. 'So, if the police can't or won't do anything, then I'm going to start doing some detective work of my own!'

Twenty

Sarah looked at the note her mother had left. 'Would someone please get a bag of sugar from the shop. Today!' The word 'Today' had been heavily underlined. As she was washing up her cereal bowl, the mail van drove up.

'Turning out nice,' the postwoman said, handing her a letter. 'Enjoying the holidays?'

Sarah nodded. 'Very much, thanks.'

The woman clucked her tongue. 'Lucky for some,' she said. 'Wish I was back at school. The best years of your life, they say.'

Sarah shook her head. 'Not any more. Too many exams.' And she stood in the doorway watching the little red van drive off. The letter was for her mother. It was from the building society she'd had an interview with. Sarah put it in the middle of the table beside the sugar bowl, to make sure she'd see it. Then she wondered where Steve had got to.

She went upstairs and peeked in at Tom. Good! He was still asleep. She didn't want him around. Not this morning. She needed space to think. The police were so pathetic about catching the baiters. It made her really angry. Sergeant Clegg had said they needed to catch the men red-handed. But, how they could hope to do so if they didn't even have enough people to watch the airfield? They wouldn't catch anybody at this rate and more badgers would certainly die.

She decided she'd walk to the village shop and fetch the sugar. It was a good mile but walking always made her think better. Outside, the air smelt fresh. A stiff breeze rustled the trees. It had rained hard during the night and there were puddles everywhere. The hedgerows glinted in the morning sun and there were birds singing. Her spirits rose.

She reached the shop and casually scanned

the notices displayed in the window. A card caught her eye and she gasped out loud. She couldn't help it. Ellis's name was written in block capitals. Underneath it, he had printed, 'Everything and Anything Repaired'. Then came his telephone number and address. 'Myrtle Cottage,' she read. She felt her chest tighten as she remembered the small stone house with the slate roof.

As she pushed open the shop door, a little bell tinkled. Everyone inside turned to see who it was. She knew them all. She set her face in a fixed smile and answered their questions about school, and being on holiday, and how Tom was doing. She wondered why adults always asked the same questions. They were so predictable. And boring. She bought the sugar and a few small items for herself. And left.

Outside, she looked at the display board again. The garage where Ellis worked was around the next corner. She hesitated, remembering the promise she and Tom had given not to have anything more to do with the baiters. But this was different. She just wanted to get another look at the man. There was no harm in that, surely?

She walked down the street towards the garage. It had a corrugated iron roof and a concrete floor, blackened by years of oil spills. An old car with a 'For Sale' sign in the windscreen was parked at one end. Ellis's van stood opposite. She recognised it at once. As she got closer, she noticed his dog sitting on the passenger's seat.

'All right for some!' a man's voice called. She looked round and her heart leapt. Ellis was walking towards her, carrying a bag of tools. He wore a pair of dirty coveralls. 'Remember me?' he called, smiling at her. 'I was at your place fixing your dad's trailer.'

That voice! How could she ever forget it! It WAS him! The man at the airfield. She knew that now with every fibre of her being. And he was looking at her. Waiting for her to reply. She must say something. Anything! Her heart thumped. He must hear it and guess!

'Like a lift? I'm going your way. Got a job to do, a couple of miles beyond.'

Somehow, Sarah managed a smile. 'I like walking,' she heard herself say. It sounded totally unconvincing. 'What's your dog's name?' she asked in desperation.

'Chico,' Ellis told her. 'And worth his weight in gold, he is.'

He dumped the tool bag behind the passenger's seat and got in. As he drove away, she saw the wheel arches were caked with mud. By then she had recovered some of her poise and gave him a guilty half-wave.

As she watched him drive away, a strange idea came to her. One that sent a cold shiver up her spine. It was crazy notion. Dangerous too. In fact, terrifying. She walked slowly past the garage and on down the road. His cottage, she knew, was along here. She was just taking a different way home, she told herself.

As she approached it, she slackened pace. There was no sign of the van. She walked past the little front garden, watching the windows from the corner of her eye. The place seemed empty. Casually, she looked back over her shoulder. The road was deserted.

She looked left and right, then she was running along the outside of the hedge. She found a gap and squatted down. No one called after her. No one came running to see what she was doing. She hugged herself and watched.

After a couple of minutes, a cat appeared and sat on the stone path outside the back door. The cat began to groom itself, then looked up and saw her. Their eyes met. The cat's mouth opened in a silent miaow. Sarah was certain there was no one there. Positive.

She hid the plastic shopping bag in some long grass and ducked through the hedge into the garden. As she approached the cat, it ran off. She was in the open now, clearly visible to anyone in the back of the cottage. She knew she should have invented an excuse for being here. And felt sick because she hadn't. She tried to think of one as she hurried up the path but by then her mind was spinning. And it was too late.

She hesitated, then knocked loudly and listened to the sound fading away inside.

Boldly, she tried the back door and found it locked, as she knew it would be. She let out her breath and for a moment felt giddy with relief. It was all right now to walk away. She looked down and saw the flowerpot. It had been moved recently. She could see the marks of its rim in the damp soil. She stooped and lifted it and saw the key lying there. Her hand trembled as she fitted it in the lock.

She stood on the threshold of the cottage, poised for flight. She had no idea what she was looking for. Or even how to recognise it if she ever found it. All she knew was that she was in the grip of a compulsion to do something. Or at least try.

It was very still inside. There were only two rooms downstairs. She went into the kitchen first. It stank of cigarette smoke. The furniture was sparse. A small wooden table and two chairs. There were milk rings on the tabletop and an electricity bill. A torn envelope lay on the floor beside a chair leg. A bowl and plate were stacked in the sink.

The tiny sitting room contained a sofa, a

television, an old-fashioned desk and, beside it, a telephone on a low table. There were four colour prints of dogs hanging on the walls and a dog basket in the corner.

Something touched her leg and she very nearly screamed. The cat stalked past her and sank its claws into the end of the sofa and ripped down. Furious, she stamped her foot at the cat and chased it out of the room. That made her feel a little better. She peered out of the window but no one seemed to have heard. She could feel the silence settling back.

She went to the foot of the stairs and looked up. She could see two closed doors. She swallowed and made herself climb upwards, step by step. She reached the landing and held her breath. But there were no upraised voices demanding to know who was there. No one strode to a bedroom door and flung it open. She wanted to look inside the rooms but then her nerve broke, and she fled downstairs. There was no one there, though. She was satisfied. The cottage was quite empty.

She went back into the sitting room. There

were two pigeonholes inside the desk, both stuffed full of papers. She stared at them blankly. Where to start? She pulled out a handful and leafed through them. They were mainly old bills and some mail order catalogues. She pushed them back. She closed the lid and bent to open the drawer underneath. Inside, there was a pad of paper and some biros. Nothing.

But when she tried to close it, it jammed halfway. She tugged it back out and tried again. The wood was warped. It stuck again. She swore out loud. If she couldn't get it to close, Ellis would know at once that someone had been going through his things. He couldn't fail to!

She put one hand at the back of the desk. Took a very deep breath and rammed the drawer shut with the other. She stood up in triumph and knocked a small glass paperweight off the desktop. It landed with a crack on top of the telephone answering machine and rolled on to the floor. As it did so, the machine clicked on.

The first message was from a woman. She sounded cross and flirtatious in turn. The other was from a man. As soon as she heard his voice, Sarah knew she had struck gold. She had found what she'd been looking for. The man's voice filled the room. It was confident and aggressive. The message was short and to the point. 'Ed! We're on for the 29th? Give us a call!'

The machine switched off. It didn't seem to have been damaged. She knelt and put the paperweight back. She was in a hurry now. Anything to get out of this place. The walls of the cottage were closing in on her. She thought she heard someone at the back door. And gave a little cry. She stood motionless, waiting to be discovered. The door creaked again and she realised it was just the wind, playing with it. Her hands shook as she locked it and she took great care to put the flowerpot back, exactly as she had found it. She crossed the tiny lawn in a couple of strides, scooped up her shopping and ran.

All the way home, she played the message to

and fro across her mind. The 29th! There was no doubt what it meant. But it was so soon! It was Saturday! This Saturday coming. Which meant the police had only five days to act.

Twenty-one

By the time Sarah reached home, some of her elation had faded. Thoughtfully, she scanned the yard for any sign of her father but the Land-Rover was not there. Good! She knew she was being a coward, but she hated rows or any sort of confrontation. She had done the right thing. There was no question about that. Now the police could act. But she still had to face her parents and tell them.

It all depended on what sort of mood they were in. Steve could be very intimidating, especially if anyone thwarted him. She had promised them, she wouldn't get involved any more. But now, this. She had literally been a spy in the enemy's camp. She did not relish having to face Mum, either. Her parents could both be really mean when they wanted to.

She thought about Sergeant Clegg. She was disappointed with him. Perhaps he would really act fast, now. She thought of the baiters being arrested and the badgers who would be saved. And that was all because of her. That was what she had done! That was what was important. Nothing else mattered. 'Yes!' she said out loud. 'Yes!' And felt good again.

Tom was in the kitchen. He looked grumpy. 'Where've you been? I've been waiting here for hours.'

'Where's Dad?'

'He's gone to give Jack Jones a hand, pick up some feed sacks or something. He wouldn't even wait for me,' Tom said crossly.

'When's he back?'

Tom shrugged. 'He said, suppertime. Why?'

Sarah didn't reply. She picked up the telephone. So it was going to have to be Sergeant Clegg after all, she thought. She found the number and dialled, ignoring Tom's questions. But Clegg was not there. 'It's urgent!' she told them. 'Very urgent! I know when the badger baiters are meeting! It's this Saturday, tell him! He knows who I am!'

'It's his day off,' she told an open-mouthed Tom, as she banged the phone down. 'They don't know where he is and they won't give me his mobile number. They'll tell him the next time he calls in!'

She rang the police station again at teatime but without any luck. Tom was out in the yard talking to Eric. She watched them, hoping to goodness Tom would keep his promise not to tell. She was certain he would. He was good like that. She went up to her room to read but it was hopeless. She could not concentrate. Increasingly, she kept turning to look at her alarm clock. She began to pace up and down. Why didn't Clegg call her?

A long hour later, she heard the sound of her father's Land-Rover hooting as it came up the track. That sounded positive, she thought, rushing downstairs. She opened the kitchen door and Buster leapt up at her, licking her hands in delight. She pushed him away and he went skidding across the tiled floor, anxious to see if anything had dropped into his food bowl while he'd been away.

Steve came bustling in, with Tom at his heels. He kissed her on the cheek and gave her a quick hug. 'Mum not back?'

'She's here now!' Tom called, staying outside to greet her. Buster started to bark. Steve put the kettle on. Tom brought in a shopping bag and Sarah began to lay the table for supper. She remembered the letter that had come earlier that morning. 'It's for you,' she told her mother, handing it to her.

Joyce turned it over and opened it with her finger. She gave a cry, her eyes wide with surprise. 'It's from that building society! Listen! "The person originally selected for this post has had to resign due to personal reasons," ' she read out loud. ' "Would you still be interested in the position that again exists at this branch?" '

'Would I?' she whooped, twirling round and waving the letter high above her head. Steve grabbed her by the shoulders and danced her the length of the kitchen. Tom looked at Sarah and rolled his eyes. Then he grinned and made sick-making gestures. Sarah smiled back and tried to remember when she had last seen her parents so happy.

'Mum! If you get this job, will there be a lot more money?' Tom asked.

Joyce laughed. 'You bet there will!' She looked at Steve. 'Enough to make all the difference!'

'Good!' Tom told her. 'Then we'll all be happier.'

'How d'you mean?' Steve asked.

Tom nudged Sarah. Joyce saw him and looked puzzled.

'Come on, Mum!' Sarah protested. 'It's been a bad time for both of you.'

'Like you arguing,' Tom interrupted. 'And looking miserable most of the time.'

'We're not stupid,' Sarah added. 'We notice things.'

Steve and Joyce looked embarrassed.

'Well, thanks for telling us,' Joyce laughed. 'We're sorry!'

The phone rang. 'It's for me,' Sarah thought, as Steve picked it up. She watched his face. He held it out to her, frowning.

'It's Sergeant Clegg. For you!'

The only way to go now was forward. She cleared her throat, nervously, aware of the silence in the room behind her. She could feel them staring at her, listening. When she finished, Clegg asked to speak to Steve.

Sarah sat down beside Tom. She felt his arm against hers. It was something. Steve put the phone back in its cradle.

Joyce broke the tension. 'Sarah! How could you? You promised us!'

Steve sat down at the head of the table. He looked shaken. 'You went into Ellis's house? Right inside it?'

'I think she's been very brave,' Tom cried.

'Very stupid!' Steve scowled. 'What if he'd come in?'

She shook her head impatiently. 'He was going out to do a job. I watched him drive off. He offered me a lift back here.'

Joyce clicked her tongue. 'Silly girl!'

'Then I was passing his cottage and there was no one about. Well, you heard me tell Sergeant Clegg.' She looked at her parents, silently pleading with them to understand. 'I didn't mean to do it on purpose. It just sort of happened.' Her voice died away.

Steve spoke to Joyce. 'Clegg's going to have a word with her when it's all over.'

'Well, I hope he's got more influence over her than I have!'

'Oh, God!' Sarah thought.

'Well anyway,' said Tom, defiantly, 'she's got the information the police needed. I think they should give her a medal!' He glared round. 'Now the police can catch those men and put them in prison. I think it's brilliant!'

There was a silence. A lop-sided grin began to spread across Steve's face. 'You know what?' he told Tom. 'You're right! I do too. In gold.' He waved a finger at his wife. 'She's just like you! Can't stick injustice. People getting away with it. Bullies!'

'I don't want to hear anything more about any of this. She was very lucky! All I can say is, roll on Saturday!' Joyce told them. 'Then all this nonsense can end.'

Steve went to the door and took his old jacket from its peg. 'Maybe. But that's a few days away. It's not over yet.'

Sarah heard the concern in his voice. He was outside now, pulling on his boots.

'What's worrying you, Dad?'

He put his head back round the door. 'I'll tell you what's worrying me. Ellis knows we've got badgers on our land. And where they are. So if he's got to find one in a hurry, what's the betting he'll know just where to start digging?'

Horrified, the twins stared at each other.

'I'm going up there now,' Steve told them. 'It's almost dusk. Anyone want to watch 'em coming out to feed?'

'Your suppers will be on the table in one hour's time,' Joyce called after them. She closed the door and sighed. What a day! Oh well! It wouldn't be long until Saturday. And next week, she could hand in her notice to that smug little manager. She smiled, broadly. She couldn't wait to see his face!

Twenty-two

The storm came on the Friday. A big one. Marla stood motionless outside the sett, listening to the wind rushing through the wood. She could smell the sea on its breath and knew it would get worse. There was a malevolence in its strength that brought memories of previous storms crowding to the front of her mind. Of trees torn out by the roots and flung aside, of the sett flooded with storm water and tunnels collapsing.

There was a brilliant flash, a deafening bang and the ground shuddered under her feet. The air hissed and crackled and stank of burnt electricity. Every hair of her body stood on end. She screamed and rushed blindly for the entrance and tumbled in.

She collided with Cadoc and, panic-stricken, tried to force a way past as the thunder rolled over them. They snarled at each other and bared their teeth in fright. Each one biting at the other's jaw, desperate to get away. They heard the roar of the approaching rain. Cadoc turned and hurried away. Marla followed at his heels. There would be no foraging for either of them tonight.

The wind beat at the Jefersons' farmhouse, rattling the doors, tugging at the windows, seeking a way in. Up in the roof, a slate worked loose. The wind howled in triumph and flung it high over the chimney pots. It blew the dustbins over and sent them clattering across the yard. They fetched up against the side of a barn, and rolled there from side to side until morning. Out in the fields, the cattle huddled together for comfort. They stood with their backs to the wind, their heads hanging in resignation, as the rain lashed them.

'It's forked lightning!' Steve warned, peering out. 'Turn the TV off. Don't want that burning out.' He took his long, waterproof coat off its hook and shook it out. He began to put it on.

Sarah looked at him in amazement. 'Where are you off to, Dad?'

'Nowhere!' said Joyce, getting to her feet.

'We checked the barns and things an hour ago!' Tom protested.

Steve shook his head and looked at his wife. 'This storm's going to last all night and most of tomorrow. I'd better check on the badgers before it gets any worse.' He grinned round at them. 'Anyone want to come?'

They stared at him in disbelief. 'You're joking!' Tom exclaimed.

'You'll be hit by lightning. Or a tree. Or something!' Sarah gasped.

Buster closed his eyes, huddled down deeper into his basket and pretended to be asleep. But Joyce was not in the least bit fazed. She turned on the outside lights. 'Now, tell me what you see?' she said with mock brightness. 'Remind you of anything? A monsoon, perhaps?' She put her hands on his shoulders and began pulling off his coat.

'You're not going anywhere. No one's going to be disturbing your badgers on a night like this. Now are they?'

But she was wrong.

The van stopped close to a row of beech trees. The driver's window jerked down. 'This is it,' said Ellis, peering out. 'We'll park up under those trees.'

The other man grunted and looked at the swaying curtain of rain beyond the headlights. 'And get bogged in!' he said irritably.

Ellis shook his head. 'There's hard-standing there. An old Roman road or some such. Trust me. I've been here before.' The van pulled off the little road that ran over the back of the hill and Ellis switched off the engine. The two men sat in the darkness drinking coffee from a flask, listening to the rain drumming on the roof. 'No one's going to be out in this,' Ellis said with satisfaction.

'What about that farmer of yours?' his passenger asked.

Ellis smiled. 'You mean Jeferson? He was out here the other night with his kids. But he won't be out in this.' He stubbed out a cigarette. 'Got more sense. Right now, he'll be at home. Nice and warm.'

'Wish we were!' the other man said bitterly.

A small, sturdy dog emerged from the back of the van. It yawned and stood with its paws on the seat behind Ellis, staring at the rain. Then it leaned down and licked the side of his face. Ellis rubbed its ears. 'Got some action tonight, Chico!'

'This rain's never going to stop,' the passenger grumbled.

'You're dead right!' Ellis told him cheerfully. 'So the sooner we start, the quicker we get finished. Come on, then! Time to go!' The dog barked and ran to the rear doors. It started scratching at them. The men got out.

Ellis put the dog on a lead, then picked up a spade. 'You got the collar and the box of tricks?' he shouted into the passenger's ear. The man gave him a thumbs-up. Ellis nodded. 'And don't forget the pickaxe.'

Cadoc lay outside the chamber he shared with Marla and shivered. He was guarding the sett from the storm raging outside. Protecting the family from the stabs of lightning and the terrifying shaking of thunder. The storm frightened Cadoc. All around him, he could hear tree roots straining as they fought to keep a hold on the stones and boulders underground. He could feel their distress and trembled at the strength of the wind that was tearing them bodily out of the earth.

Marla was somewhere deep inside the sett but he didn't know where. She had disappeared some time ago, taking the rest of the family with her. He was glad they'd gone. The cubs' howling had been unsettling. He lay with his chin on his paws and listened to the rain splashing in the tunnel entrance. He closed his eyes and thought about food. He thought of all the slugs that would appear when the storm was over and this cheered him. He licked his lips and never heard the dog coming. Just caught the smell of its breath at the last moment.

He reared up as the dog's teeth tore at his nose. The pain took his breath away. For a moment, he was blinded by tears. He shook his head to clear them and swatted the dog with his paw. The dog sidestepped easily and came at him again. Its little eyes blazing with hate. And overconfidence.

Cadoc's long claws reached out and slashed the dog's side. The dog yelped and stumbled and lost its concentration. It struggled for breath, shocked by the force of the blow. Cadoc charged, his mouth wide open. The dog backed rapidly away and began to bark.

Ellis lay full-length at the entrance to the sett, his head and shoulders wedged tight inside. He shouted encouragement while the rain and sand poured down his neck. The dog heard him and barked louder. It stayed just out of reach of Cadoc, jumping back in the nick of time, dodging the badger's claws and teeth. And all the time it kept up its relentless barking. A nagging, merciless sound that tormented the badger. It was a weapon of finely tuned agony developed to perfection in the dog, by generations of specialized breeding.

Cadoc knew perfectly well why the dog was barking. It was telling the men where he was. He hated all dogs. They were humans' allies. If he could only seize it in his jaws, he could put an end to its hideous barking, for ever! He wondered what the men were doing.

The thump of spades overhead told him. Cadoc backed away. The dog came after him barking in triumph. Almost hysterical. Sand and loose earth filtered down from the roof of the tunnel. Some landed on the dog's head, distracting it. In that split second, Cadoc lunged. Too late, the dog sensed the danger and leapt back. But by then, Cadoc had him by the leg. The badger's great jaws closed. The dog's barking faltered and changed to a scream. Cadoc shook his head from side to side, his jaws grinding together.

A steel blade cut through the roof just above their heads. The dog sobbed to its master for help. And went on crying. Now there were steel blades everywhere, slicing down through the earth, reaching towards the badger. The air was full of dust. Cadoc dropped the dog and backed away. But still the dog would not give up. It stood balancing on one front leg, baring its teeth at Cadoc, and whimpering for the men to come quickly. They did.

A brilliant light blazed down. Cadoc froze. Blinded. The dog staggered towards him, snarling weakly, desperate to show his love of his master. Cadoc heard the men's voices. Felt them jumping down beside him. Smelt them. And could do nothing. The light burned into his brain, paralysing him. He could not see. He could not think. He was helpless.

A blow on the head made him stagger. Strong hands gripped him by the tail and heaved him upwards. He snarled and tried to twist away. His head and shoulders were thrust inside a sack. Then he was dropping down into a darkness that stank of blood and fear.

Cadoc felt their arms tighten around his body. The next moment, they were lifting him up. Then they were walking, lurching from side to side. Every step taking him away from the family and the life he had known.

Twenty-three

It was still blowing hard early next morning when Steve reached the sett. He stood stock-still, rigid with horror, staring at the gaping hole and the torn ground. In sheer disbelief, he knelt down and peered inside, his face crumpling at the tragedy. There was nothing to see. Just raindrops splashing into the puddles on the tunnel floor.

He sat on his haunches and gazed around. The men's footmarks had long ago filled with water. There had been two of them. He could see their tracks stretching across the bare earth and back into the wood. He stood up and tried to follow them but it was hopeless. Once in the wood, they immediately disappeared into the carpet of sodden leaves.

There was a loud crack behind him. He spun round, his fists held high in front of him. But it was only a branch breaking in the wind. He shook his head; his nerves were getting the better of him. This was crazy. These people had outwitted him, totally. They had guessed he wouldn't come last night. Perhaps they were watching him? He looked over his shoulder, then very quickly all round him, in case someone was slow ducking down.

And then anger exploded inside him. He shouted into the wind, cursing Ellis and all the men who had done this. How dare they! This was his land. His family had farmed it for over a century. They had shared this hillside with badgers throughout that time. And the sett had been here, a hundred years before that. And now this! This violation of that trust. Well, they'd picked the wrong man to cross. There was no way Ellis and his cronies were going to beat him. No way! Even if he had to take them all on single-handed.

He turned and trudged back to the Land-Rover, hate raging through him. But his mind was clear. First, he must telephone the police. Then, bring the family up here and show them what had happened. This was very personal now.

Later that morning, the phone rang in the kitchen. Joyce picked it up. 'It's for you,' she said, handing Steve the receiver. 'Your friend the police sergeant.'

Steve took it eagerly. But slowly, the expression on his face began to change. He turned away so that his back was towards them. His voice thickened. 'So, are you on for tonight or not?' The twins looked at each other in alarm. Joyce went to put her hand on his shoulder but he waved her away.

He was shouting now. 'And if I was to go round to his cottage now and confront him, I'd probably be the one ending up in jail! Is that it?' They could hear Clegg replying. Steve listened for a few moments more, then banged the phone down on him. 'Wonderful!' he said sarcastically. 'Just wonderful!'

'What's happened?' they demanded.

'What's gone wrong!' Sarah cried.

'That was our friend, Sergeant Clegg,' he told them, in a voice not quite under control. 'The good news is that the police will TRY and be there tonight . . . But . . . there's no guarantee. Apparently, they've discussed it and his superintendent is all for it. However, the bad news is that as it's a Saturday night, they might not have enough resources to spare! And if that's the case, they'll all be terribly sorry!'

'Oh, Steve! That's dreadful!' said Joyce, holding out her arms.

He buried his face in her neck, very close to tears, and they stood hugging each other. 'So that's that!' he said. His face had gone very red. 'Those poor badgers! God! I'd love to take a baseball bat to that man so he knows that it feels like!'

He looked at Sarah and Tom. 'And all that brave work you put in. I'm sorry. What a waste!' He walked past them to the door, not meeting their gaze. 'I'm going out for a bit,' he mumbled. 'Just around the farm.'

They watched him go.

Lunch was a silent affair. Afterwards, Mrs Jeferson drove on her own into town, to do the weekly shop. The twins hung around the farm, moodily waiting for time to pass. They thought of cycling down to the village. But what if they bumped into Ellis?

As the afternoon wore on, Steve's mood changed. Sarah noticed the difference first. She decided he had made up his mind about something. But what? She could tell by the way he walked that his confidence was returning. He spent some time in the Land-Rover, taking things out and rummaging in the back. She even saw him kneeling down, peering at the rear lights.

'He's up to something,' she told Tom. 'He's got a plan. I know it!'

At teatime, Steve rang the police station again. He listened impassively. 'They're still saying how much they want to raid the airfield.

But it all depends on what happens in the town. Blah! Blah! Blah!'

'Do you believe them?' asked Tom.

He sucked at his teeth. 'I suppose so. But there's always trouble on a Saturday night. Why can't they use a little imagination and go for something like this? It would make all the difference to animal crime if they caught these people.'

After supper, he went off to the pub, leaving the others watching television. Tom went to bed that night feeling utterly wretched. All he could think of was the airfield. And those men. And the last time they had been there. To his surprise, he fell asleep almost at once.

Twenty-four

Sarah crossed the landing on tiptoe. She pushed open Tom's bedroom door and bent over him. 'Tom! Tom! Wake up!' she breathed, shaking his shoulder. 'Wake up, Tom!'

Tom gave a startled grunt and sat bolt upright. 'What's the matter? What's up?'

She put her hand over his mouth. 'Keep your voice down!' she hissed. She was very tense. Somewhere in the house, a wooden beam creaked. But there was no sound of her mother's door opening.

Tom pushed her hand away and reached for the bedside light. 'What's the time?'

She screwed up her eyes against the glare. 'Almost midnight.'

'What's happened?'

'Dad's up to something!'

Tom yawned and lay back on his pillow. 'Like what?' His eyes began to close.

She shook him, harder this time. 'Wake up! Listen! He came back to the barn to get something. He was parked at the end of the track. I heard him. Now he's gone again.'

'Why? Where's he gone?'

Sarah frowned. 'Isn't it obvious?'

Tom's jaw dropped. 'You don't mean the airfield! You're joking!'

She shook her head, impatiently. 'You know what he's like! Now the police have let us down and everything, I told you he had a plan.'

Tom was thoroughly awake now. 'He's crazy! You're telling me he's out there on his own. With all those men!' He swung his legs out of bed. 'We've got to do something!'

'We promised we'd keep out of it! Remember?'

Tom reached for his shirt. 'That was when the police were going to help. This is different!'

'All right!' said Sarah simply. 'So what do we do?'

Tom said nothing for a moment. He was thinking of Steve and what the men would do to him if they caught him. 'I don't know what we do. But we've got to be there. Just in case we can help.' He stared at her and there was a hardness to his face that she had never seen before. 'Get dressed!'

Outside, the night was warm and full of clouds, scudding along. The storm had almost blown itself out. They cycled in silence, each busy with their own fears. It was a lot further than Sarah remembered. This time, they dismounted a long way short of the hole in the fence.

Tom put a hand on her arm and they waited, motionless, listening and staring into the night. An age crawled past before Tom was satisfied no one had heard or seen them arrive. Walking very slowly, they followed the fence until they found the gap.

The grass was still wet from the storm and the legs of their jeans were soaking by the time they squeezed through. This time, there was no moon. The ground in front of them was cloaked in darkness and from where they stood, there was no sign of the buildings. Keeping very close, the twins hurried on.

Cadoc licked the moisture from the side of the sack. His throat was dry and cracked, and hurt when he swallowed. His tongue was swollen and kept sticking to the roof of his mouth. But it was the heat that was draining him of life. His coat was heavy with sweat. It ran into his eyes and nostrils. He lay motionless, enduring it. His breath coming in shallow gasps, each one adding to the steaming humidity in there.

He knew there was another badger close by. Earlier, during the day, they had called to one another and attacked the sacks that imprisoned them in a frenzy of biting and slashing. Their bodies bumped and rolled against each other as they fought to get free. Now, they lay in silence. Defeated. Listening to the growing volume of noise outside the van. And trembling.

There were dogs out there. The type of dog Cadoc had learned to dread. He thought there were six of them. He lifted his head and stared into the blackness, listening, knowing what their barking meant. The badger beside him snarled and tried to turn around to face them.

There were men everywhere. Their feet thudding across the ground. Coming nearer. Their voices harsh and loud. A dog was pleading to be let off the leash. Cadoc could hear its claws scratching at the bumper bar. The rear doors were flung open. Hands reached in and dragged a sack out. Cadoc screamed in terror as the doors banged shut.

Steve knelt beside the furthest building and watched the men through night glasses. He thought there were ten of them. Add on the two men he had spotted on the road and that made a dozen. And he knew, there'd be more inside. Long odds! He wondered if the men on the road would be coming up to join the fun. Best assume so. He'd have to watch his back the whole time.

He shifted position and scanned behind him. There was no sign of any movement there.

The night glasses were good. The best he could afford. He had used them scores of times to watch badgers and foxes but never for anything like this.

He watched the men gathering round the van. Someone switched on a flashlight and shone it inside. He saw them dragging out a long bundle and knew there was a badger inside. It might be one of them from his sett! He thought there was another shape lying there on the floor, but couldn't be sure. It would make sense if there was. The men had brought a lot of dogs with them so they were clearly expecting plenty of 'sport'!

He recognised Ellis immediately and felt his anger flare up. Ellis hoisted the sack on to his shoulder. The men crowded after him and disappeared inside. A flicker of movement caught his eye. He raised his glasses. There was a man on top of the steps running up the outside of the building. He was looking down at Ellis's van. Steve cursed silently. Another lookout. The man lit a cigarette. It glowed briefly, then he turned away.

From inside, Steve heard a muffled cheer, then individual voices shouting. Now he could hear a dog yelping. He shivered, remembering the twins' description, and imagining what must be happening. He wished now he had told Clegg he was coming out here. That had been a mistake. The men's voices rose, howling encouragement, and for the first time that night, Steve felt afraid.

The man on the steps was moving! Steve held his breath, willing him on. The man's boots began to clump down the steps. He tossed his cigarette away. It hit the tarmac and flickered out. At the foot of the stairs, he looked around, then opened a door and slipped inside.

Steve did not hesitate. This was the chance he had been praying for. He was out in the open like a flash, bent double and racing towards the van. He thought he heard a shout a long way behind him but by then, he was only a few metres from it.

He threw back the doors and reached inside. His hands closed over a sack and he felt the badger moving under them. A wild elation seized him. He laughed out loud and lifted it up. The badger slipped to the other end. Its weight took him by surprise and wrong-footed him. He staggered and fell against the van to steady himself.

Then he was off, running clumsily, with the sack in his arms. But someone was challenging him. Starting to run towards him. Two of them. Shouting at him to stop. The men at the entrance! He had forgotten all about them!

He dodged between two small buildings and ran out into the darkness. The ground was uneven, covered with old bricks and debris. He tripped and fell, knocking the breath from his body. The badger screamed in panic.

Other voices were shouting. He guessed the man on the steps was one of them. Steve pushed himself back up and looked around, searching for a hiding place. He saw the sagging door of the hut next to him. It wasn't much but it was all there was. He stooped, grabbed the sack and dragged it towards the door. There was a chance, just a chance, he might be able to come back and find it. A torch flashed on. And another. Probing the darkness for him. Shouts of anger. Very near. They were coming at him from the side. Steve swerved and ran for dear life.

Fifty metres away, Tom hugged the ground and knew it was the end. It had to be. The men must see him. They were so close. Sarah was somewhere near by but he didn't dare look around. The men were cursing and gasping for breath. Chasing after someone. One of them was trying to talk into a mobile.

He heard boots squelching in the mud and the laboured sound of breathing. Moments later, two dark figures ran past and he caught the smell of stale beer. There was more shouting in front of him. A lot more. Growing louder all the time. He guessed the men were all pouring out of the building.

'Tom! Tom!' Sarah was bending over him, pummelling him with her fists. 'Get up! That's Dad they're after! And he had a badger. I saw him drop it. It's over here! Come on!'

He ran after her, barely understanding what she was saying. 'Where is it?' Her voice was shrill with panic. 'It's here! I know it is!'

'There's something moving!' he cried. 'I can hear it! Over there! By the door!'

She pushed past him with a little cry and knelt down. 'It's the badger! It's here! Come on! Help me!'

He tried to swing the sack over his shoulder and staggered back. 'Give me a hand! Quick! Up on my shoulder!' He tried to run after her. The badger's weight was crushing his lungs. 'Where're you going?' he gasped.

'The road!' she cried. 'Dad must have parked along there, somewhere. Come on!'

Tom's heart sank. It was a long way to the road. He tightened his grip on the sack and forced himself to follow. His foot slipped and the sack rolled off his shoulder. 'Give me a hand!' he begged. They carried the sack between them, running awkwardly. Each stumble making the badger slide around. The muscles in their arms were on fire. Time had no meaning. All their concentration was centred on keeping the sack level while they struggled on.

There was a hoarse shout behind them. 'They're kids! Just kids!'

'Get them!' a voice ordered. Sarah recognized it immediately. Ellis!

She saw his face in her imagination. Coming nearer and nearer. She was living in a bad dream. The worst kind of nightmare. The one where you're running through treacle and know you can't escape. The ground sucked at her feet, pulling her back. Everything was slowing down. She couldn't make her legs go any faster. And the sack was as heavy as lead. She sobbed out loud. She couldn't go on much longer. It would all end in misery. Or something worse.

There were boots pounding after them and others running to cut them off. Men were all around them. She could hear them breathing and cursing her. Sarah tripped and almost fell. The sack slipped from her grasp. It began to bump across the ground. She saw Tom's mouth open in a helpless shout. She screamed. And went on screaming as Ellis grabbed her. She knew it was him long before he knocked her down.

And as she rolled over and over, she saw the flash of headlights in front of her. Headlights coming towards them. And the sound of engines. Ellis was straightening up, his hands on the sack. Cursing. Staring into the headlights. Headlights that roared towards them. Blinding them. Blue lights began to flash. Sirens wailed. Ellis scrambled up and ran into a night full of confusion and panic.

And hope. Two police cars roared past. Sarah stared after them. Doors were flung open and uniformed men tumbled out. Another car braked to a halt in front of them. A burly figure loomed up in the headlights. A disbelieving voice shouted, 'What the hell are you kids doing here?' It was Sergeant Clegg.

'We've got a badger!' Tom gasped. 'In this sack!'

'And Dad's here!' Sarah cried. 'The men were chasing him.'

'He's out on the airfield!' Tom shouted.

Sergeant Clegg glared at them. 'You stay right here! Understand! Both of you. Don't move an inch till I get back. Or I'll arrest you myself!' Then he put a hand on both their shoulders. 'Well done!' And there was sudden warmth in his voice.

Twenty-five

'Who's next for a bacon sandwich?' Joyce Jeferson asked, looking round.

'It's got your name on it, love,' Steve told her. 'Come and sit down and join us.'

'I'll put some more toast on,' she told them. 'Though why I'm being so nice, I can't think. You're all as bad as each other!'

They were in the Jeferson kitchen, sitting round the table and wolfing down a very early breakfast. A police car stood outside. It had brought the twins back, a half-hour ago.

Sergeant Clegg grinned at her. 'Joyce! You've got a family of heroes. Every one of them!'

'Family of idiots, more like! And I can't decide who's the worst. That great lump of a husband of mine, who should know better at his age, or these children, who never, ever do what they promise.' She clicked her tongue. 'Can't trust any of them.'

Steve winked at the twins. Tom grinned back. Sarah stifled a yawn and thought longingly of her bed. Joyce studied them, critically. They looked drawn and tired with deep shadows under their eyes. Steve's face was bruised and he walked stiffly, with a limp in one leg. For him too, the police had got there in the nick of time.

Joyce touched his cheek. 'I'll put some more witch-hazel on that, after breakfast.'

He shook his head. 'It'll be all right in a day or two. No need to make a fuss.'

'Make a fuss? Me!' she exclaimed. 'You've got a nerve! I'm the most patient woman in the world.' She folded her arms. 'So, now that you've all been fed, perhaps someone can tell me what the heck's been going on!' She pointed at Sergeant Clegg. 'Starting with you!'

They all looked at the policeman.

'You said you weren't coming,' Tom reminded him.

'Yes! Come on, Pete!' Steve agreed. 'Why the sudden change of plan? If I'd known you were going to raid the place, I'd never have gone to the airfield.'

'Neither would the twins!' exclaimed Joyce. 'I hope!'

'Would have saved me this,' said Steve, patting his leg.

Clegg bowed his head. 'Fair enough! And you're right! We weren't going to do anything almost up to the last moment, like I told you.' He caught Tom's eye. 'Well, we couldn't. There wasn't a spare constable to be had, let alone a squad car.'

'So why the sudden change?' Steve asked.

Clegg spread his hands. 'Forensic! Forensic made your badgers top priority.' And seeing their frowns, he went on. 'Steve! Remember I told you I had a friend at the police laboratory? Well, she worked overtime and a half yesterday to examine that dead badger. The one we found in the ditch.'

'The lampers,' Steve reminded them.

'That's the one. It had been shot with a handgun,' Clegg told Joyce. 'And guess what she found when she checked out the bullets?' He paused, knowing they were hanging on his words. 'They were from a pistol that had recently been used in a gangland killing. A drug dealer in Manchester.'

'Oh my God!' cried Joyce. 'And my family were mixed up with these people!'

The twins stared at each other.

'Go on, Pete!' Steve insisted.

'Well, all of a sudden we were now part of an ongoing murder inquiry. And a big one at that. The powers that be pulled out all the stops and got to the airfield in double-quick time. Luckily for you!'

The Jefersons digested the news in silence. Buster put his head on Steve's knee. And was pushed away. He went back to his basket and flopped down with a sigh.

'Have they got the man who fired the gun?' Sarah asked.

Clegg shook his head. 'They're doing the

tests now, so we won't know for another day. But there's every chance this will nail him. Thanks to all of you, we're expecting to make an arrest, very shortly.'

'How many men did you get at the airfield?' Tom demanded.

'You caught Ellis!' Sarah cried. 'I saw him in handcuffs.' She gave a little shiver. 'He saw me, watching him.'

'We picked up seventeen,' Clegg told them. 'Red-handed. Some more got away in the darkness but we're on to them. There was a freshly killed badger in that room they were using.'

Steve's chair scraped. 'Hey! That reminds me! Come on!' he called. 'We've got to get our badger back home.'

'How d'you know he's yours?' Joyce demanded.

Steve grinned. 'Because I know! I've spent enough time watching him. He's got a nick out of one ear. And he's the head of the family. Nice-looking fellow. Like me!'

'He's in the yard, in a cage we brought,'

Sergeant Clegg told her. 'He's got water, he'll be OK.'

Tom grinned. 'And I gave him some apples. I found a couple in the old shed. I knew you wouldn't mind, Mum.' They all laughed.

Sergeant Clegg raised his voice. 'There is just one thing, before we go. I'd like to say a few words to these two young people. And it's something I think needs saying!'

Joyce looked at the twins and then at Steve, in alarm.

The policeman hesitated. 'I know the chief constable will be writing to thank you,' he began. 'But, there's one thing, I'd like to say to you, personally.'

He looked at the twins. 'I've been in the Force for ten years now. And in all that time, I've never known anything quite like what you two have done. What you did was dangerous. Very dangerous. It almost went horribly wrong. But by a miracle, it didn't!'

He took a deep breath. Sarah saw his hand was trembling. 'Thank you! Thank you on behalf of all the decent people out there.

Thank you, for having the guts to do what you did!'

There was a lump in Tom's throat. He looked away and saw Sarah blink back tears. Joyce was on her feet, hugging them all in turn. 'You daft idiots!' she mumbled. Then she was reaching for her handkerchief

Steve cleared his throat and headed for the door. 'I'll get the Land-Rover.' His voice sounded gruff. 'Then we can all squash in.'

Marla heard them coming and grew even more agitated. She chased the cubs away and stood in the old sleeping chamber, listening. She knew that humans had taken Cadoc away. Their scent was everywhere. And the dog's. Earlier, she had made the cubs smell both carefully so they would never forget. Now, they were coming back for her. Climbing the hill, towards the sett.

They were outside now. A lot of them. She could hear them whispering and muttering. They were excited. She could smell it. Her coat bristled and her mouth opened in a snarl.

There was a strange scraping noise and a loud sigh from the humans. Then, footfalls running towards her. Getting louder. And a familiar scent that made her whimper. The next moment, Cadoc was beside her, licking her face and making baby noises. His teeth gripped her lower jaw and she growled in pleasure and bit his ear, in welcome.

She heard the humans leaving but was too engrossed to care.